while it lasts

ALSO BY ABBI GLINES

The Vincent Boys
The Vincent Brothers

Other Sea Breeze Novels
Breathe
Because of Low
Just for Now

while it lasts

ABBI GLINES

Simon Pulse

New York   London   Toronto   Sydney   New Delhi

SIMON PULSE

An imprint of Simon & Schuster Children's Publishing Division

1230 Avenue of the Americas, New York, NY 10020

First Simon Pulse edition August 2013

Copyright © 2012 by Abbi Glines

All rights reserved, including the right of reproduction in whole or in part in any form.

SIMON PULSE and colophon are registered trademarks of Simon & Schuster, Inc.

For information about special discounts for bulk purchases, please contact Simon & Schuster Special Sales at 1-866-506-1949 or business@simonandschuster.com.

The Simon & Schuster Speakers Bureau can bring authors to your live event. For more information or to book an event contact the Simon & Schuster Speakers Bureau at 1-866-248-3049 or visit our website at www.simonspeakers.com.

Designed by Mike Rosamilia

The text of this book was set in Adobe Caslon Pro.

Manufactured in the United States of America

2 4 6 8 10 9 7 5 3 1

This book has been cataloged with the Library of Congress.

ISBN 978-1-4424-8867-0 (hc)

ISBN 978-1-4424-8866-3 (pbk)

ISBN 978-1-4424-8868-7 (eBook)

This one is for my FP girls.
You know who you are and you know
that I love you something crazy.
There are some things you can only say
to the ones who can understand . . .
and you girls understand.

ACKNOWLEDGMENTS

I have to start by thanking Keith, my husband, who tolerated the dirty house, the lack of clean clothes, and my mood swings while I wrote this book (and all my other books).

My three precious kiddos, who ate a lot of corn dogs, pizza, and Frosted Flakes because I was locked away writing. I promise, I cooked them many good hot meals once I finished.

Tammara Webber, Elizabeth Reyes, and Liz Reinhardt, my critique partners. Somehow I convinced these ladies to become my critique partners. Now I get to read their books before anyone else! I'd throw in an "I'm just kidding," but, well . . . I'm not. I love their work. It's a major perk. They all helped me so much with *While It Lasts*. Their ideas, suggestions, and encouragement made the writing process so much easier. They're amazing, and I don't know how I ever finished a book without them.

My FP girls. I'm choosing not to share what "FP" stands for because my mother may read this, and it will give her heart failure. Kidding . . . maybe. You girls make me laugh, listen to me vent, and always manage to give me some eye candy to make my day brighter. You are truly my posse. What happens in New York City stays in New York City . . . eh, girls?

Prologue

"Your mom brought me the letter today." The pain in my chest was so sharp I had to fight to keep from bending over and screaming. "I read every last word. Several times."

The autumn wind caressed my face but wasn't enough to dry my tears. The tears were endless. Never ceasing. Swallowing hard, I forced myself to continue. I needed him to hear me. "It isn't fair, you know. . . . A letter isn't the proper way to say goodbye. It sucks, Josh. It sucks so damn bad." A sob tore from my chest. I pressed my fist against my heart. How much more pain could it take before it just exploded into a million pieces?

"You always told me we'd grow old together. We'd sit on our front porch swing, holding hands and watching our grandkids play in the yard. You promised me that," I choked out as I pressed my thumb against the tiny diamond solitaire that he'd placed on my finger just six months ago.

"You broke your promise. You've never broken a promise before. This time you let me down and left me this letter. How do I move on from this, huh? Did you expect me to just read it and everything would be better? Did you expect me to cry a few tears, then move on?" I would get no response. Nothing more than the letter weighing heavily in my back pocket. It was so tear stained now that several of the words were hard to read. Didn't matter, though. I had it all memorized. Every. Last. Word.

"I started to write you a letter and bring it to you today. My chance at a few last words—but I couldn't. I can't scream and yell in a letter. Words on paper can't hold the emotions churning inside me." I reached into my pocket and pulled out the worn letter that would haunt me for the rest of my life.

"Instead of writing you a letter, I decided I'd respond to yours in person. It's only fair. No . . . it isn't fair," I spat out angrily, "because none of this is fair, but this is all I get. This is all you allowed me to have."

I opened the one-page letter carefully. I didn't want to tear it because the words written on it were all I had left. I began to read aloud:

"'My Eva Blue.'" Fresh tears streamed down my face. Just reading the nickname Josh had given me when we were nine years old was painful. How could I read this entire letter aloud without crumbling to the ground?

"'The fact that I'm writing this letter pains me more than

you could ever know. This isn't something I ever want you to read, but I know that you deserve a good-bye. You deserve so much more than that, and God willing, you will get the perfect life that we've spent hours together daydreaming about.'" I stopped reading and lifted my eyes from the words on the paper.

"We made those plans, Josh. You and me. Those aren't just my plans. They're our plans, damn you! How could you just leave me? We had it all figured out. All those nights spent lying under the stars, choosing the names of our children, the color of our bedroom, the flowers we'd plant in the pots on our front porch, the summer house we'd have on the beach—ALL THAT WAS US!"

Another tear rolled down my face and I quickly swiped it away with my hand before it could drop onto the paper below. I had to finish this. As hard as reading this was, I had to finish it. This would never be closure. I'd never get closure. This would be the closest thing I'd ever get to a good-bye.

"'I've loved you since the moment I looked into those pretty blue eyes of yours. Even at five years old, I knew there'd never be a girl who could take your place in my heart. No one would ever compare to you. It would always be you for me, Eva Brooks. Always. Please remember that: You were all that ever mattered to me. No one else ever touched my heart the way you did. My life was marked with every year I grew more and more in love with the wild, crazy, beautiful girl next door. I lived in awe that this perfect angel wanted me, that this amazing woman would be my wife. The life we planned, the life we dreamed about was what kept me going as long as I did." Sinking to the ground, I pulled my knees against my chest and sobbed as I forced my eyes to focus on the words I had to read. I had to. I had to.

"'I pray to God you never have to read this letter. I want this to be a letter I pull out of my box one day for you to read when we are old and gray. We can smile and realize how much we have to be thankful for because this letter was never needed. But, Eva, if you do receive this letter from my mom one day, then know: I loved you until my last breath. You were the only thing on my mind when I closed my eyes the last time. Our time together was more perfect than anyone's life should be. The life I lived was heaven on earth because I spent it with you.'"

"Oh, God, Josh, I can't do this without you! I can't do this without you. I love you so much. Please, please, God." I wept loudly. No one heard me. The graveyard was empty. The last few lines of the letter were the most impossible to accept. How could he even think that his words were possible?

"'One day you will heal. Life will go on for you. Another guy will be lucky enough to find a place in your heart. When that happens, love him. Move on. Live that life of happiness that you deserve. Know that I loved you. Know that you made my life complete. But move on, Eva. Love again. Live your life. Love, Josh.'"

Chapter One

Eighteen months later . . .

CAGE

"Thanks for giving me a ride," I said, reaching for my duffel bag holding my entire summer wardrobe.

"I did it for Low," Marcus Hardy reminded me for the second time. My best friend, Willow, was a chick—a smoking-hot chick. Marcus, her fiancé, was an elitist ass at times, but I dealt with him. Had to if I wanted to keep Low in my life. All that mattered was that he understood that Low walked on fucking water. As long as he kept that in mind and treated her as such, I could live with the prick.

"I never questioned that," I replied with a smirk, pulling the straps of my bag up onto my shoulder. Turning my attention from Marcus, I looked at the large white-and-tan farmhouse in front of me. It was surrounded by miles and miles of green grass, trees, and a helluva lot of cows—my purgatory for the entire summer. Glancing back at Marcus, I nodded and started to close the door. I knew he was ready to get back to Sea Breeze, where Low was waiting on him. No one wanted to be stuck in this fucking cow town.

"Cage. Wait," Marcus called out before I could completely close the truck door. Slowly, I opened it back up and arched an eyebrow in question. What else could Marcus want with me? He'd barely spoken to me on the hour's ride up here.

"Don't screw this up, okay? Stay sober. Don't drive a car until you get your license back, and try not to piss off your coach's brother. Your future is riding on this summer, and you're upsetting Low. I don't want her worried about you. Think about someone other than yourself for a change." Well, hell, I'd just got a parental lecture from Marcus fucking Hardy. Wasn't that sweet?

"I know what happens if I screw things up, Marcus. Thanks for the reminder, though." I let the sarcasm drip from my voice.

Marcus frowned and started to say something more before just shaking his head and putting his truck in reverse. Conversation over. Good. The guy should learn to mind his own damn business.

I slammed the door and turned my attention back to the house while Marcus's tires spun out of the gravel drive. Guess I'd better go meet my warden for the rest of the summer and get this party started. All I had to do was make this guy happy.

I'd take care of his cows and do manual labor for two and a half months, and then my coach wouldn't kick my ass off the baseball team. The DUI he'd had to bail me out of jail for would be forgotten and my baseball scholarship would remain intact. I only had three problems with this plan:

1. No girls.

2. I hated manual labor.

3. No girls.

Other than that, this wasn't all that bad. I'd get Sundays off. I'd just have to get my fill of sexy little sorority girls in tiny bikinis on Sundays. I reached the front door of the house. The wraparound porch was pretty damn nice. I wasn't into the farm thing, but this place wasn't half bad. I bet the bedrooms were a nice size.

"You must be the fella Wilson hired for the summer." A guy in a pair of faded jeans and some worn-looking, badass boots started up the steps of the porch. He was smiling like he was really glad to see me. Must be the guy's son. I'd be shoveling hay and cow shit all summer instead of him. Bet he liked me a lot.

"Yeah," I replied, "Cage York. Coach Mack sent me."

The guy grinned and nodded, sticking both his hands into his front pockets. All he needed was a damn piece of straw hanging out of his mouth to look like every stereotypical country boy.

"Ah, that's right. I heard about you. DUI. Man, that sucks. 'Specially since Wilson is a damn slave driver. My brother and

I worked many a summer for him through high school. I swear you'll never drink and drive again."

Guess he wasn't the old man's kid after all. Nodding, I turned to knock on the door.

"Wilson ain't back from the stockyard yet. He'll be here in 'bout an hour." The guy held out his hand. "I'm Jeremy Beasley, by the way. I reckon we'll see enough of each other over the summer, seeing as I'm the next-door neighbor. And, well, then there is Eva." He stopped and his eyes shifted from me to the door. I started to ask him who Eva was when I followed his gaze to find the light at the end of the tunnel standing in the doorway.

Long brown hair that curled loosely was draped over one bare shoulder. The clearest blue eyes I'd ever seen, framed by long, thick black eyelashes and full red lips, completed the perfect masterpiece of her face. My gaze slowly traveled south to take in smooth, tanned skin that was barely covered by a bikini top and a pair of tiny shorts that hung on her narrow hips. Then legs. Legs for miles and miles until two small bare feet with red toenails finished the fucking ridiculously perfect package in front of me. Damn. Maybe I should have come out to the country more often. I didn't realize they grew girls like this out here.

"Eva, you aren't ready yet? I thought we were going to make the six thirty show," Jeremy said from behind me. Ah, hell no. Surely not. This goddess was with that guy? I brought my eyes back up to her face to find her blue eyes staring directly at me. They really were the bluest damn eyes I'd ever seen.

"Who are you?" The icy tone to her voice confused me.

"Down, girl. Play nice, Eva. This is the guy your daddy has helping him this summer." Her eyes flashed something that looked like disgust. Really? I'd seen that look in a girl's eyes, but never before I'd used her and then tossed her. Interesting.

"You're the drunk," she stated.

It wasn't a question. So I didn't reply. Instead I flashed her a smile that I knew affected any female's panties and took a step toward her. "I got a lot of names, baby," I finally responded.

Her eyebrows arched, and she straightened her stance and shot me the coldest glare I'd ever witnessed. What was this chick's deal? "I'm sure you do. Let me guess: STD, Loser, Jackass, and Drunk, just to name a few," she clipped, stepping out of the door and slamming it behind her. She swung her gaze to Jeremy, who I could have sworn just chuckled.

"I can't make the movie, Jer. I need you to ride over to Mrs. Mabel's with me and help me get her well working again. It needs to be primed."

"Again?"

"Yes, again. She really needs a new one."

Eva walked past me, grabbed Jeremy's arm, and pulled him toward the stairs. Apparently, I had been dismissed.

"Has your dad called her boys yet? They need to get their

asses down here and help their momma," Jeremy said as they started walking away without a backward glance.

What the hell? Who just walks off and leaves a guy standing on their porch without a word? She was one insanely gorgeous but crazy-ass bitch.

"Hey, do I just go inside?" I called out.

Eva stopped and spun around. The same disgusted expression was on her face as before. "The house? Uh, no," she replied with a shake of her head like I was crazy. She lifted her hand and pointed toward the two-story red barn that was located back behind the house. "Your room is in the back of the barn. It has a bed and a shower."

Well, wasn't that just fucking fantastic . . . ?

EVA

I hated guys like Cage. Life was a joke to him. There was no doubt in my mind that females of all ages drooled at his feet. He was healthy, alive, and throwing it all away like it was a game.

"Pull in the claws, sweetheart. You got your point across. He won't come sniffing 'round you again." Jeremy reached over and squeezed my leg gently, then turned on the radio.

"He's a jerk," I said through clenched teeth.

Jeremy let out a low laugh and shifted in his seat. I knew

he was deciding on how to respond to me. The only other person who had known me as well as or better than Jeremy did was Josh—his twin brother and my fiancé. We'd all grown up together. Jeremy had always been the odd one out, but Josh and I had done our best to include him as much as possible.

When Josh had been killed by a bomb just north of Baghdad eighteen months ago, the only person I could stand to have near me had been Jeremy. Josh and Jeremy's momma said it was because Jeremy was the only one I felt could understand my grief. In a way, we'd both lost our other half.

"And how'd you get that outta the brief conversation we just had with him? Seemed like a nice guy to me." Jeremy was always optimistic. He always saw the best in people. It was up to me to keep people from taking advantage of his trusting spirit. Josh wasn't here to do that anymore.

"He's here because he was drinking and driving, Jer. That isn't exactly a small offense. He could have hit a family. He could have killed someone's kid. He's a selfish loser." Who really was too good-looking to be real. I'd have to get over that, though. His pretty face wouldn't get to me.

"Eva, lots of people drink and drive a little. He probably was just going a short distance from the bar to his house. I doubt he was on a road trip. Probably just had a couple of beers."

Sweet Jeremy. Bless his heart, he had no idea how depraved some people were. It was one of the things I loved about him. I happened to know Cage York was lit up like the Fourth of July when he had been pulled over. I'd heard Uncle Mack talk about what a thug he was and how the only thing he ever took seriously was baseball.

"Trust me, Jer, that guy is trouble."

Jeremy didn't respond. He leaned his elbow on the open window and let the warm breeze cool him down. The inside of Daddy's farm truck was smoldering hot this time of year, but it was the only vehicle I'd drive. My vehicle sat in the garage, untouched. I couldn't bring myself to drive it, and I couldn't bring myself to get rid of it. The pretty silver Jeep that Daddy had bought me hadn't been driven since I'd gotten the call from Josh's momma telling me he'd been killed. Josh had proposed to me in that Jeep, overlooking Hollows Grove. Then he'd turned the music up on the radio and we'd gotten out and danced under the stars. I hadn't laid eyes on it in a year and a half. Instead I drove the farm truck. It was just easier.

"Eva?" Jeremy asked, breaking into my memories. He always seemed to know when I needed someone to stop me from remembering.

"Yeah?"

"You know I love you, right?"

Tensing, I gripped the steering wheel tightly. When Jeremy started with something like that, I never liked what he was going to say next. Last time he'd asked me that, the next thing he'd said was that I should really start driving my Jeep again because Josh would want me to.

"Don't, Jer," I replied.

"It's time to take the ring off, Eva."

My hands stung from the death grip I had on the worn steering wheel. The gold band on my finger dug into my skin, reminding me it was there. I'd never taken it off. I never would.

"Jeremy, don't."

He let out a long, heavy sigh and shook his head. I waited patiently for him to say more and was so thankful when we pulled into Mrs. Mabel's. I all but jumped out of the truck before it came to a complete stop in my determination to get away from him before he could say anything else. The engagement ring Josh had put on my finger couldn't be removed. It would be as if I was forgetting him. Like I was moving on and leaving him behind. I'd never leave him behind.

Chapter Two

CAGE

This could not be my room. It was the size of the closet in my bedroom at my apartment. I dropped my duffel down onto the twin bed that sat crammed in the corner of the tiny room. On the opposite side, a small, round bedside table barely had enough space to fit between the side of the bed and the wall. Then, at the other end of the narrow room, was a shower. The cement floor had a drain in the far corner and a small showerhead came out of the wall. A dark-blue shower curtain hanging from a simple rod was the only barrier between the shower and the bed. I was pretty sure if I got too carried away in the shower, I'd get the bed wet. My phone started ringing in my pocket, and I pulled it out to see Low's name lighting up the screen.

"Hey, baby," I replied, backing up and sinking down onto the bed. Surprisingly, the mattress wasn't bad.

"So how is everything? Are they nice?" Just hearing Low's voice made me feel better—not so alone.

"I've only met the guy's daughter and the next-door neighbor."

"Oh, so there's a farmer's daughter?" The teasing tone in Low's voice made me chuckle. Yeah, there was a farmer's daughter all right, but it wasn't what Low was thinking.

"There's a farmer's daughter, but she hated me on sight. Crazy, I know. And to think, I thought it was impossible for a female to hate me until after I bagged her and then forgot her name in the morning."

"She hates you? That's . . . odd." Low's voice trailed off like she was deep in thought.

The loud sound of the barn door swinging open caught my attention.

"Low, I gotta go, baby. I think the old man's here."

"Okay, be on your best behavior."

"Always," I replied before hanging up and slipping my phone back into my pocket.

"Hello?" a deep, husky voice called out.

I walked out of the small broom closet they'd stuck me in and headed for the sound of his voice. As I turned the corner, I stopped short. The dude was huge. At least six foot seven, and three hundred pounds of hard muscle. The straw cowboy hat cocked back on his head showed that he was completely bald.

"You Cage York?" he asked. His serious expression reminded me a lot of Coach, but that was as far as the similarities went. Coach was not this fucking massive.

"Yeah," I replied, and the man's eyes narrowed, and he took a step toward me. It took every last bit of my self-control not to back the hell up.

"Boy, your daddy ever tell you it's rude not to respect your elders? I expect any kid your age to respond to me with a 'Yes, sir.' That understood?"

Really? What the hell was Coach thinking? This would never work.

"When I ask you a question, I expect a response," the giant growled.

Fine. I'd give him a fucking response. "No."

His frown grew deeper, and annoyance flickered in his eyes. I had a lot riding on this damn job, but I wasn't one to handle this kind of shit well.

"No, what?" he asked in a slow drawl.

"No, my daddy didn't teach me anything but that his fuck-ing fists were bigger than my momma's and how to skip out on your family," I replied with a sneer in my voice.

The angry scowl on his face didn't change. I hadn't expected it to, but then I also hadn't expected to tell the man my personal shit. It had just come out. My family was something I'd only ever talked about with Low, and that had been when we were younger and it still affected me.

I watched as he reached up and rubbed the scruff on his jaw, never once taking his eyes off me. I was ready for this meeting to be over with and for him to tell me what it was I was supposed to do exactly.

"Mack wants to help you. I trust his judgment. But listen here and listen good. I ain't above kicking your ass off my property if you do any drugs or drive a vehicle while drinking. That was stupid, kid. Beyond stupid. And most importantly, stay away from my little girl. She's completely off-limits to you. Got that?"

Considering Eva had hated me on sight, the man had nothing to worry about. Besides, no girl was worth fucking up my future. Not when there were so many other willing, available females in the world I could enjoy.

"Got it. I don't want to lose my scholarship," I replied with complete honesty.

With a nod of his head, he stuck his large hand out toward me. "In that case, I'm Wilson Brooks. Now let's get your ass to work."

EVA

"Boy ain't got no dad. Those are the kinds you stay away from," Daddy said in way of greeting as he opened the screen door and walked into the kitchen. I rolled my eyes as I went back to battering the chicken breasts I was going to fry for dinner.

"I mean it, Eva. He ain't had the same upbringing you had, and he's cocky, with no respect for authority. Just rubs me the wrong way." Daddy set his hat down on the table and walked over to fix himself a glass of sweet iced tea.

"I wasn't impressed by him. Stop preaching at me. I'm not on the hunt for a man." I'd never date again. I had Jeremy, and until he met a girl and fell in love, I would have a companion to do things with. The familiar pang in my chest reminded me that I held him back from a life. I hated that he put everything else aside to take care of me. He was always so worried about me. I knew for a fact that Chelsea Jacobson had a crush on him. I really needed to do something to push him in her direction.

"Hmph," Daddy mumbled as he sat down at the end of the kitchen table. "I know you aren't looking for a guy, Eva girl, but honey, you're a woman. One day you're going to have to open your heart again."

"Daddy, don't, please. I just want to fry this chicken, make your favorite blueberry cobbler, and enjoy dinner. Let's not talk about anything else. Okay?"

With a deep sigh, Daddy finally nodded. He reached for his hat and placed it back on his bald head. "It's times like this I think I made a mistake not marrying again. Maybe you did need a momma after all. Because right now I don't know what to do to fix this for you, baby girl."

I laid the last piece of battered chicken on the plate and washed my hands under the faucet. Then took an extra-long time scrubbing my fingers with the soap before turning to look at my dad. "You were enough. You are enough. Don't say that anymore. I'm happy just the way things are. I don't need someone to fill Josh's place in my life. I don't want someone to fill his place. Okay?"

Daddy closed the distance between us and gave me a quick, hard hug before turning and leaving the kitchen through the same door he'd entered. I knew my disinterest in dating other guys and moving on bothered him, but I couldn't. I wouldn't. Josh had been my future. Now he was gone.

The door swung back open behind me. I wasn't expecting Jeremy tonight for dinner, but I'd made enough just in case.

It wasn't Jeremy. It was him.

Cage held up his hands as if to say he came in peace. The easy smile from earlier was gone. He wasn't looking at me like he wanted to take a bite, either. Instead he looked disinterested.

"I just need a drink. Your dad sent me in here and said to ask you. But I can see you're busy, so if you'd point me to the glasses, I'll get my own water."

Was this the same guy from earlier? I forced myself not to

continue gawking at him, and I turned to get a glass out of the cabinet. I handed it to him. "I keep a pitcher of ice water in the fridge. We have well water here, and water from a well tastes better when it's really cold."

He nodded. "Thanks."

I turned back around and checked the temperature of the oil on the stove.

The sound of Cage gulping down the water had images flashing in my head of how his throat muscles would move with each swallow. I closed my eyes tightly, trying to stop my imagination. I listened as he opened the fridge and poured himself some more water. Then once again he drank it quickly. The silence in the kitchen only intensified the sound of his drinking.

"That's better. I was fu— uh—really thirsty. Thanks for the glass and the water." Cage sighed and walked to the sink. "You want me to wash it, or is that something you'd rather do?"

"Uh, I can get it," I stammered, still completely thrown off balance by his behavior.

"Thanks. But I don't mind washing it."

"No, really, I can do it. I'll just rinse it and stick it in the dishwasher anyway." I was rambling.

The kitchen door swung open again, and I was so thankful for the interruption until Becca Lynn came bouncing into the house, all blond curls and smiles. Normally, I enjoyed Becca's bubbly interruptions in my life, but not now. Not when Cage was standing here. Becca was an idiot when it came to attractive guys, and Cage York went beyond attractive.

Her big brown eyes slowly took him in. I cleared my throat, trying to get her attention, but she wasn't aware anyone else was in the room. The tight tank top and cutoff shorts complete with cowboy boots were Becca's summer wardrobe. It was all she ever wore, and she wore it well. I shifted my attention from Becca to Cage, whose sexy smirk had returned, and he was enjoying the view just as much as she was. I couldn't call Becca Lynn my best friend because Josh had always been my best friend. Nevertheless, she was the closest female friend I'd ever had. Where Josh and Jeremy grew up to the right of me, Becca Lynn grew up on the farm to the left of me. So when I'd needed a partner in crime who wasn't male, it had been Becca. She and Jeremy had once had a thing back during our sophomore year of high school. I was pretty sure she'd been the one to take his virginity. But it was short lived. Jeremy had ended it without an explanation, and Becca Lynn had cried on my shoulder for a few days and then moved on the next week to Benji Fitz.

"You didn't tell me you had company, Eva," Becca Lynn cooed, twirling one of her long blond locks around her finger while batting her eyelashes in Cage's direction. Good Lord, she was ridiculous.

"I don't have company, Becca," I retorted, hoping to get her attention, but it didn't work. "This is Daddy's summer help. He's working with our cows. Because he got a DUI and he's serving time." Maybe that would snap her up out of her worshipful gaze. It didn't.

"Oh, so you'll be here all summer?" she asked, still smiling up at Cage like he was a freaking rock star.

"Looks that way," he replied in an amused tone. Great, even the man whore beside me thought she was making a fool of herself.

"Well, when you're not working and get bored, I could keep you company—"

"Becca Lynn." I raised my voice to stop her from offering to come warm his damn bed in the barn.

Finally her eyes shifted off Cage to meet my gaze. The twinkle in her eyes told me she knew exactly how it sounded and she didn't care one bit.

"Thank you. I'm sure that I'll be needing someone to show me what to do for entertainment when the workday is through. I can't think of anyone else I'd rather have take me around and enlighten me about the things to do out here in the country." The sexy drawl thing he had going on just pissed me off. It also gave me goose bumps and made my heart race.

Becca Lynn's eyes swung back over to eat Cage alive. "That sounds like a really good plan," she cooed, closing the distance between them and holding out her perfectly manicured hand. I was sure the hot-pink nails that she wiggled in his direction invitingly matched her toenails. Becca was as high maintenance as they came around here. "I'm Becca Lynn Blevins."

Cage stepped closer and slipped his hand into hers. Did Becca just shiver? "Cage York, and it's a pleasure, Becca."

"Oh." She breathed out, her head tilted back as she drank him in. I swear, if he kissed her in my kitchen, I was going to throw my cobbler batter at him.

"I got to get back to work. I'll be looking for you to come entertain me soon, Becca Lynn," Cage said in a low whisper, then stepped around her and headed out the door without a backward glance.

The second the door closed behind him, Becca pulled out a kitchen chair and sank down into it with a loud thump. "OHMYGOD!" she squealed. "I swear I think I just creamed my damn panties."

Cringing from the mental image, I shook my head and made a gagging noise. "I was ready for you to lie on my table and spread your legs for him right here. You really need to get a grip on yourself, Becca. You came off as a complete slut."

Becca let out a loud sigh. "Oh, who cares! He was the most incredibly delicious male specimen I have ever laid my eyes on. I want to marry him and have his babies and wash his body and dress him, and hell, Eva, I just want to touch his body all day long. I could do it the rest of my life and never grow tired."

Before I could think of a response that would hopefully be a source of wisdom for her, the door swung open again and Jeremy walked inside. His presence eased me. Just the familiar face that was so much like his brother's helped remind me I'd had it all once. Jeremy's eyes found Becca sitting at the table with the dazed expression still on her face. A knowing grin touched his lips.

"I see Becca Lynn met Cage."

I nodded and dropped a chicken breast into the oil, which was finally bubbling.

"I bet he ate you up, Becca. Poor boy got a rude welcome from Eva earlier. Having a female actually drool over him must have been nice for his ego."

Jeremy would have to bring that up.

"You were rude to *that* piece of perfection?" Becca Lynn asked incredulously.

I focused on frying the chicken in front of me. I wasn't going to talk about this. "You two staying for dinner?" I asked instead.

"Is he eating dinner with you?" Becca Lynn asked hopefully.

"Of course not. He's the help. Besides, Daddy isn't a fan of his. I'll fix him a plate and send it out to the barn."

"MEMEMEME! Can I take it out to him?" Becca asked. I didn't have to look back to know she was bouncing up and down in her seat.

An image of Cage York with his shirt off, pressing Becca up against the wall and actually putting his hands on her, had me shaking my head.

"Daddy won't like that. I'll have Jeremy take it." I was sure Daddy wouldn't really care who took it as long as it wasn't me. For some reason, the idea of Becca touching Cage bothered me. I wasn't sure why exactly, but it did. The idea of my friend pregnant and unmarried with a loser as the baby daddy was probably the main reason.

Chapter Three

CAGE

Those damn cows came running when I showed up with the feed. They actually knew it was chow time and I had the goods. It was also scary as shit to have those sons of bitches running at me like they were going to trample me. Wiping my forehead with the towel Wilson had left me this morning saying I'd need it soon enough, I sat down on the tailgate of the truck and reached for the thermos of ice water he'd also brought me. It was almost gone. It had to be at least ninety-five degrees already today and it wasn't even lunchtime. I'd been hoping the little blonde with the boots would show up today and give me a brief distraction. She seemed like the easy kind. The no-strings-attached sort. I needed to blow off some steam. Especially if I was going to have to watch Eva

Brooks strut around in a bikini top and tiny shorts all damn day. Reminding myself that she was completely off-limits was difficult.

Eva wasn't the first girl I'd had to refuse myself. I'd refused to touch Low, but for different reasons. She was my best friend. I respected her. I wanted to know that when we moved into a relationship that included sex, that she would be my only one. That had never happened. Honestly, I doubted it ever would have. Even if Marcus hadn't come along. I just wasn't a one-woman guy.

The difference with Eva was that the only reason I wasn't touching her was because her daddy would hang me up by my nuts and then fire my ass, and I could kiss my scholarship good-bye. Well, that and the girl really didn't seem to like me much. But I wanted a taste of her. Bad. Real bad. She had such a hot little temper, it would be fun to see what she was like during sex. Shaking my head, I stood up and reached for my towel to tuck it into my back pocket. I wondered if I'd even be thinking about her if she wasn't so off-limits. The whole "wanting what you can't have" thing always did bug the hell out of me.

"You ready to go bale some hay?" Jeremy asked as he walked up beside the truck.

"Not really, but I don't think I get a choice," I replied with a grin. He was a nice guy. Eva probably led him around by his nose, because he was too damn nice for someone like her.

She needed a strong hand. Someone she couldn't push around. Someone who wasn't afraid to tie her ass up and—stop! I had to quit thinking about her. She was the "do not touch" toy.

"It ain't all that bad. Besides, we can always go jump in the lake and cool off. It's the only way to make it all day in this heat."

I'd seen the lake yesterday when Wilson had taken me around in his truck to show me the property. The lake was man-made and ran along the back of three properties. The Beasleys', which were Jeremy's folks, this one, and the Blevins'. Hot little Becca Lynn's family. I could think of some fun activities Becca Lynn and I could entertain ourselves with in that lake.

"I'm out of water. I need more before we go."

Jeremy glanced back at the house, then at me. "Mind if I go get it for you?"

I could hear the apologetic tone in his voice. That was weird. Was he sorry that his girl disliked me so much? Most guys would be thrilled.

"Not at all. I'm sure Eva would prefer you go get it."

Jeremy sighed. "Yeah, she would."

These country folks were weird and oddly polite. I thought I'd handled Eva well yesterday afternoon in the kitchen.

Jeremy chuckled and snapped me out of my Eva thoughts. "Looks like you got company anyway."

Becca Lynn was strutting toward us in another tight tank

top. This one was pink. Pale pink. And the girl didn't have on a bra. Wow. She wasn't playing around. Yeah, Becca Lynn and I would get along just fine.

"I'll be back in a few," Jeremy said before heading up toward the house.

Becca Lynn stopped in front of me and cocked her hip to one side, placing her hands in the back pockets of her cutoff jean shorts. That stance made her tits poke out, and the imprint of her nipples was right there for my viewing pleasure.

"So you getting a break anytime soon?" she asked, staring up at me with a "fuck me now" grin on her face. I was real damn tempted. I could have those tight little shorts off and her bent over my bed in no time. But something was stopping me. Maybe it was the innocent way her blond curls floated around her big brown eyes, or maybe it wasn't something that moral at all. Maybe it was the fact that she'd be harder to get rid of out here in the country once I'd finished with her.

"I'm heading out to bale hay. Jeremy just went to get us some water," I explained, making sure she understood just how disappointed I was that I wouldn't get to see exactly what those perky little titties looked like bare.

"Oh . . . well, maybe tonight you would like to come down to the lake? I'm having a bonfire and inviting over a few friends. My parents are out of town. . . ." She trailed off. Not getting some sexual relief from this pretty little number was going to be hard. But I wasn't going to turn down her offer of something to do tonight. I was already bored as shit.

"I'm in need of a nice, cold beer. Any chance that'll be available?" I asked.

Becca nodded and bit down on her bottom lip teasingly. Yeah, she was hoping for more tonight. Maybe if I just enjoyed having a female in my arms for a little while . . . No sex, just some playtime. I fucking needed something.

I checked to see if Eva or her dad were standing around anywhere watching us before closing the little bit of distance Becca Lynn had left between us. "That sounds like a real nice offer." I lowered my voice and placed a hand on her hip. Her mouth made a little round O as I pulled her up against me. "Do you think you might could sit on my lap while I drink that beer?"

Her breathing was accelerating, and the tits she wanted me to notice were bobbing against my chest. I slid my hand up her ribs until my thumb grazed the underside of her soft, heavy breast. Yeah, that was nice. I needed to get fucking laid. She managed to nod as she stared up at me. Her brown eyes were pretty, but not enough to put up with a clingy female the rest of the summer. That reminder had me slipping my hand away and taking a step back.

"I'll see ya tonight then," I replied, suddenly thankful that Jeremy was headed our way.

"Okay." She sighed and flashed me one last smile before

turning and running up toward the house. Shit. I wondered if she was going to go tell Eva about this. I hadn't done anything wrong. Maybe Eva wouldn't go running off to her daddy to tell him that I was playing with Becca Lynn's tits. But somehow ... I seriously doubted it.

EVA

My face felt hot. I stepped away from the bathroom window and closed my eyes tightly. When I'd seen Becca strutting up to Cage, I should have stopped washing my hands and turned away from the window. No. When I'd realized Cage was shirtless and pouring the last of his water over his bare chest, I should have stopped looking. But I hadn't. I couldn't. It had been fascinating. I'd never seen a chest or arms like his. They were so ... so ... so sculpted and muscular. I fanned my face, glad I had a moment to recover before Becca found me in here.

Becca had been real close to that naked chest. Those large tanned hands had touched her waist, and from what I could tell, he'd touched a little more than that. I was surprised Becca hadn't crumpled to the ground. The girl didn't even have on a bra! Did she have no shame? I was torn between disgust and jealousy. Yes, I might as well admit it: I was jealous. The guy was gorgeous and Becca was free to enjoy just how gorgeous he was. I was jealous of that. Because I knew I wasn't. I'd never be free.

Even if my daddy were to approve of someone like Cage, I could never move on with someone less than worthy of filling Josh's shoes. Josh had wanted me to move on, and I wasn't sure I ever could. If I did . . . If I ever attempted to, it would have to be with a guy Josh would approve of. Cage York would never be that guy.

"EVA! WHERE ARE YOU?" Becca Lynn's voice called out down the hall as she got closer to the bathroom door I knew she would bang on any second. Taking one deep breath, I wiped my hands on the hand towel and opened the door.

Becca had just stopped outside the door and had her fist up ready to knock.

"There you are! Ohmygod, Eva! I think I'm gonna kiss your uncle Mack next time I see him. I swear my body hasn't gone this crazy over a boy ever. Cage makes me feel like I've just had the world's best orgasm when he hasn't done anything more than smile at me with those delicious full lips of his. *Dear Lord, have mercy*—his thumb touched my boob, and I'm more than positive I did have an orgasm right there in your yard." Becca pushed past me, closed the toilet lid, flopped down on it, and began fanning herself. "I am so going to do him tonight. I don't care that I just met him. I want that boy naked! Did you see him out there with his shirt off?"

Yes, I'd seen him.

"Don't have sex with him, Becca. He probably has STDs.

He will screw you today and move on to someone else tomorrow. Don't give him that part of you."

Because I was pretty sure I'd die of jealousy having to hear her relive it over and over again.

Becca Lynn rolled her eyes. "Whatever, Eva. He does not have STDs. That's silly. It isn't like he screws prostitutes. The boy can pick and choose. Besides, I will make sure we use a condom. Anyway, who else is he going to move on to? He's stuck here all summer. Other than you and me, no one else is coming around here for him to move on to."

I thought about the girls who would be at the lake party tonight and wondered if that had ever crossed her mind.

"Deedee and Farrah are coming tonight, aren't they?" I asked, leaning a hip against the sink.

Becca frowned for a moment, then lifted her gaze to meet mine. "Deedee is back with Brett, and Farrah is seeing Hayden Morris—you know the boy who was quarterback at Sea Breeze our junior and senior years. Josh outplayed him during the championship game and we . . ." She trailed off like she always did when she mentioned Josh's name. It was as though she was afraid I'd burst into tears and fall to the ground. I couldn't blame her. I had been a major recluse for over eight months after Josh was killed. Other than Jeremy, I had closed everyone out during those months. Becca had been away at college most of that time, so it hadn't been difficult to hide from everyone. Jeremy had dropped out that semester, and I'd been so wrapped up in my pain that I hadn't thought about how my grief was affecting him. When I'd heard my dad talking to Jeremy one night after he thought I'd gone to bed, I realized what I was doing to him. Dad had been telling him that he needed to go back to school that fall. He couldn't stay here with me forever. Jeremy had refused to leave me.

I'd done everything I could to prove to him that I was better. That I could make it without him. In the end it had been pointless. He'd enrolled at a local college and he commuted. By the winter semester, I'd enrolled too. We had commuted together. It had worked.

This was our last summer together. Things were changing. Jeremy wanted to go to LSU. He had family in Louisiana, and he wanted to get an apartment with his cousin. He had no idea I knew all this. But I did. I was doing everything I could to prove to him that he could tell me his plans. I would be okay. It was time he lived his life and stopped holding my hand.

"I didn't mean to . . ." Becca's voice broke into my thoughts, and I realized she thought my quietness was because of her mentioning Josh.

I smiled. "It's okay to say his name. I don't want to pretend he didn't exist. I can hear his name now and not fall apart. Josh was the biggest part of my life for eighteen years. I like remembering things about him," I assured her, and reached out to squeeze her shoulder. "He was awesome that game. We were the ones picked to lose, and he dominated that field. He showed all those college scouts that the hotshot quarterback Hayden Morris wasn't so big and bad after all."

Becca's smile was sad. "Yeah, he did, didn't he? Why didn't he take that scholarship to South Carolina for football?"

My chest tightened. I wasn't ready for that just yet. Shaking my head, I straightened up from my relaxed stance. "Because he said life was more than football. He wanted his life to mean something more."

That was all I could manage. I turned and walked out the door. I needed a moment. I thought back to that day he'd left for boot camp and I'd cried my eyes out begging him not to join the army. I had promised him I would go to South Carolina with him. We wouldn't have to be apart and he'd be safe. Away from guns and bombs.

Chapter Four

CAGE

I knew enough about country music to know that it was George Strait's voice singing over the speakers. Becca Lynn's hand squeezed mine as she walked beside me toward the big-ass fire they had going. The moonlight was the only other light out here in the woods. The small area was crowded with unfamiliar faces. A couple of them I wouldn't mind getting to know a little better. A flirty little brunette flashed me a teasing smile before pressing her nice-size chest against the arm of the guy she was holding on to.

I surveyed the rest of the crowd. I still wasn't sure I was going to be doing anything with Becca Lynn tonight. I couldn't make up my mind. I just had a feeling she was going to be the kind you couldn't get rid of after the one-nighter. There were a few other options out here in the dark. My mind went to Eva, and I wondered if she'd be here. This probably wasn't her scene. I doubted Eva Brooks went to bonfires at night. But damned if the idea of getting her snobby little ass pressed up against a tree didn't sound real good. She might be a bitch, but she was so fucking sexy it didn't even matter. I'd have to keep reminding myself that she was off-limits. I had too much riding on her daddy liking me to get too attached to the idea of getting her out of her panties.

"Let me go get you that beer," Becca said, reminding me she was beside me.

"Thanks," I replied, smiling down at her.

"Here come Jeremy and Eva. You can talk to them while I'm gone." She beamed, then turned to hurry toward the large coolers full of ice sitting as far away from the fire as possible. Of course Eva had shown up with the boyfriend who didn't suit her at all. She needed someone who could show her how to loosen up. Good ol' Jeremy wasn't that guy.

"Hey, man, Becca dragged you out here tonight, huh?" Jeremy said in an amused tone as he stopped beside me.

"Yeah. I thought I'd check out the nightlife around this place," I replied, shifting my eyes from Jeremy to Eva. She wasn't looking at me, but I could tell she was trying real hard not to. Her stiff posture told me she was very aware that I was watching her. Dammit, why'd that make me fucking happy?

"Thanks for sending out the cold ice rags today. Those sure were nice," I said, knowing she wouldn't be able to ignore me now.

She took a deep breath that she tried to hide, but I was watching her too closely. Then she turned her eyes my way, and it was like a damn kick in the stomach when the light from the fire illuminated her face. I'd been with a lot of gorgeous women, but never had I been so affected by their looks before. There was something in her eyes that drew me in. I wanted to make the sadness she tried to hide go away. Eva Brooks was haunted, and my protective tendencies were being tugged on.

"You're welcome," she replied in a clipped tone.

"I realize that those were probably meant for Jeremy, but he shared and it was much appreciated."

A small frown puckered her brow. "I sent two out there, didn't I? One for each of you."

Ah, so she was admitting to thinking about me, too. I liked that.

"Really? Well, thank you. I was under the impression you wouldn't spit on me if I was on fire."

Jeremy's amused response was a low chuckle that was beginning to get on my nerves. He did that a lot.

"As long as you do the work that Daddy has for you, and you work hard, then I will be more than happy to supply you with water and cold towels."

Her responses were all so matter-of-fact. Did she ever get

passionate or emotional about anything? It would be a damn shame if she was that cool and controlled during sex. Something in her eyes told me she was holding back. There was something I was missing.

She lifted her hand to tuck a stray lock behind her ear, and I saw the twinkle of a small diamond that sat securely on her left hand. I stared at it as understanding slowly began to sink in.

Eva was engaged.

Words left me. The world tilted a little off center. I jerked my gaze off the ring to Jeremy, who was watching me closely. Jeremy was her fucking fiancé?

"Here ya go," Becca Lynn said as she held out a can of Bud Light to me. I took it from her outstretched hand and opened it, taking a very long swallow. I had to get my head on straight. I hadn't been expecting this. Jeremy and Eva dating was crazy enough, but engaged? How the hell had that happened?

"Want to go swimming?" Becca asked sweetly. I needed to remember I was here with her. I needed to focus on anything other than that diamond ring on Eva's hand.

"Sure," I managed to reply.

"Becca, don't do that." Eva's obvious disapproval surprised me. What the hell was wrong with swimming? Was she against that too?

"Why not?" Becca Lynn chirped as she began pulling her tank top over her head. *Whoa.*

"Then at least go strip in the shadows and not right here in front of everyone. Especially Jeremy. You'll make him uncomfortable."

Strip? Were we going skinny-dipping?

"It ain't like Jeremy hasn't seen me naked, Eva."

What?

"Ugh, just go undress away from us," Eva replied.

"I wasn't exactly complaining. Becca Lynn has some nice knockers," Jeremy piped in.

It came out of nowhere. I suddenly saw red.

I reached over to grab Jeremy by the collar and lifted him off his feet. "Apologize now, you stupid fucker."

Jeremy's wide-eyed expression told me I'd scared the shit out of him, but I didn't care. He was engaged. To Eva. What the hell was he doing looking at other girls' tits and talking about how nice they were in front of her? Asshole.

"I'm sorry, Becca," he croaked out.

"Not her, you idiot! Eva! Apologize. To. Eva."

Why the hell did he look confused? Was he a moron?

"Uh, sorry, Eva. I didn't mean to, uh, say that," he stammered nervously.

I felt a hand on my arm tugging at me, but the blood pounding in my ears was drowning out everything else. I turned my angry glare off Jeremy to see Eva's horrified expression as she screamed and pulled on my arm.

Focusing on her words, I took a deep breath in an attempt to calm down.

"STOP IT! STOP IT NOW, CAGE!"

Slowly, I let Jeremy down, and I watched as Eva shoved me back and went to fuss over Jeremy like she was his damn momma.

"Are you okay? He's insane. What was Uncle Mack thinking sending him here? I'm so sorry, Jer."

Jeremy shook his head and gently pushed her hands away. "Eva, I'm fine. He didn't hurt me. He was just offended by my comment and apparently thought you would be too."

Well, hell yeah. Low would have killed Marcus with her bare hands had he said something like that about another woman. Eva was not reacting properly. She was mad at me. Me. Not Jeremy.

"Because he's insane. He's a drunk and he's had too much to drink."

That was it. "Excuse me, Mother Teresa, but this is my first damn beer in three days and I've only had half of it. This is not what constitutes a drunk."

She opened her mouth to respond and snapped it closed again. Then she turned to Jeremy. "Let's go. I've had all the fun I can handle for one night."

Unable to control my mouth any longer, I had to comment. "You don't know what fun is, Eva Brooks, but, baby, I could show you a world of fun if you'd loosen up just a little bit."

Her cheeks flushed bright pink, and she stiffened her back before turning and stalking off into the dark. Jeremy shook his head and then followed her.

How was I the bad guy in this?

EVA

"Can you believe him? Is he crazy? I mean, he just snatched you up, and you let him. Take up for yourself, Jer." I was furious, and just maybe a little turned on. Cage's arms had some serious bulging muscles.

"He thinks we're engaged," Jeremy replied.

I froze.

"What?" Where had Cage gotten the idea that Jeremy and I were engaged?

Jeremy took my left hand and held it up. "You wear an engagement ring, and the only guy you are seen with is me. It's an honest mistake, Eva. He was taking up for you. Which, I gotta say, I didn't get at first. Then it dawned on me that he wasn't going all caveman possessive over Becca Lynn, but he was pissed that your fiancé had just made a suggestive comment about another woman. He was defending you."

Me?

I replayed in my head everything that had just happened. Becca had been about to strip right there in front of us. I hadn't wanted to watch Cage's appreciative gaze take in her very naked body. It had bothered me. A lot. Then Jeremy had made the comment about her nice boobs. Which I knew he really liked. He had mentioned them more than once. Then . . . then . . . Cage had lost it.

Because he thought I was engaged to Jeremy. In a weird, scary way, he was defending my honor. It was . . . sweet. Well, crap. I didn't need him doing sweet things for me. Especially weird, scary, sweet things. He could have hurt Jeremy.

"You get it now?" Jeremy asked, reminding me that he was standing there in the dark with me.

"Yeah. I get it. Although, I don't want him hurting you if he sees you with another girl. I need to straighten this out."

Jeremy nodded. "I'd appreciate that. 'Cause that dude is tough. He ain't some spoiled pretty boy. He'd mess me up good if he thought I deserved it."

"Okay. I'll go back. You can stay or go. I'm just going to take the truck home after I talk to him."

"You sure? I mean, he might opt out of skinny-dipping with Becca and want to hang out with you."

No. Cage might not be totally bad, but he was still in no way good enough. Josh would never approve.

"I'll just talk to him for a few minutes, then leave."

Jeremy sighed. "Yeah, okay."

I knew he didn't completely get it. I walked over and gave

him a quick hug before turning and heading back to the lake. The glow of the fire made it easy to get back. The crowd around the fire had dwindled, and I didn't see Cage anywhere. That meant he was at the lake. Maybe . . . naked.

Cage might not be good enough for me compared to what I'd had with Josh, but I could still appreciate the beauty of his naked body. I'd never really seen Josh completely naked. I had never seen any guy completely naked.

I headed down to the lake, staying just out of the light from the bonfire so no one saw me going down there. I didn't want people making a big deal out of the fact that Eva Brooks was going to the lake to skinny-dip, because I wasn't. Not even close.

Where the path turns around the old oak tree, I stopped and slowly peeked around the corner. The sounds of splashing and giggling were growing louder from the water only a few feet away. Was Cage out there with Becca Lynn?

"You coming, Cage?" Becca Lynn's voice was close, and I backed up farther into the shadows.

I worked hard to focus my eyes in the dark. Cage stepped out of the darkness. He reached up and threw his jeans over a low branch. The moonlight hit his backside, and I covered my mouth to keep from making a sound. Because Dear God! His butt was unbelievable. The muscles in his back moved as he walked toward the water. He had muscles in his back!

"I'll come in if you come out and get me," he drawled. His

completely naked front side faced the lake for Becca and anyone else who cared to look. He wasn't ashamed at all. He knew they were looking, and he didn't care. Then again, when your body looked like that, you wouldn't mind who saw it.

Becca Lynn walked toward him, the water droplets rolling down her bare chest and stomach. I refused to let my gaze drop any lower. Cage's hands slipped around her bare waist, and he lowered his mouth to hers. That was all I could handle. My chest had a strange new ache, and my stomach felt sick. I just wanted to go back home. I'd clear things up with Cage York another time.

Chapter Five

CAGE

Tonight had been a bust. I didn't fuck drunken innocents who I couldn't walk away from the next morning. As good as Becca Lynn had felt all nice and wet, I hadn't been able to go through with it. Her vomiting had helped make this decision much easier, because at one point I'd been real close to forgetting how annoying it could be to have a pesky female who wouldn't go away.

I stepped out of my jeans and pulled back the covers so I could crawl into my bed. The sheets weren't bad. I had expected cheap sheets since this was a barn, but they were nice. Soft. I closed my eyes and let myself imagine Eva putting the sheets on the bed for me. Her hands would be soft, or maybe she'd have calluses. She did all the housework and she cooked. Wait. I hadn't seen a mom yet. Eva had been the only woman I'd seen in that house. Had her mom died? Or just skipped out on her? Her dad loved her. That was obvious.

My phone rang and I reached for it. Low's number once again lit up the screen.

"Hey, my favorite girl," I said by way of a greeting.

"Hey, how are things?" Low replied. I could hear the smile in her voice.

"Hot, and the cows are scarier than I imagined, but my tiny bed has some really nice sheets."

"What about the girl?"

Leave it to Low not to beat around the bush. "I'm pretty sure she hates me now more than she did when she first met me."

"Why? What have you done to her?"

"I haven't done a damn thing to her. I did threaten her fiancé and rough him up a bit. Nothing serious. But the douche was talking about another girl's tits in front of Eva. It was disrespectful."

Low was silent a minute. I knew she was processing this and trying to figure out how to fix my problem.

"So she's engaged?" was her response.

"Yeah, she is, and the guy isn't a good match for her. I like him, but they just don't fit, you know?"

"Hmmm . . . I guess. But they're engaged, Cage. That makes her off-limits."

I could hear the concern in her voice. "I wasn't going to go there anyway, Low. She's off-limits for many reasons. For starters, her dad would fire me on the spot and I'd lose my scholarship."

"Okay. Well, I miss you. I'm going to be there bright and early Sunday morning to get you. Marcus is going to give us time alone for the first part of the day. Then I'll drop you at your apartment and let you catch up with everyone. Marcus will have to drive you back that evening, though, because we're keeping Larissa this weekend and I'll have been away from her most of that day. Besides, as much as Marcus loves Larissa, he'll need a break from her."

"Thanks, Low. I look forward to seeing you. Only four more days to go before my reprieve from hell."

She laughed and we said our good-byes.

Two days later. No sign of Becca Lynn, and very few glimpses of Eva. The heat was getting worse, and Jeremy wasn't around to help anymore. He was back at his farm working, and I was left to figure the rest out on my own.

A cold thermos of water magically stayed full, and an icy-cold towel appeared a couple of times a day. They always showed up on the tailgate of the farm truck I used during the day. My back was always turned or I'd gone off to piss. Was she watching me from inside? How did she know when my back was turned? Damned if the idea of her watching me from inside didn't make me smile.

I pulled my sweat-soaked shirt over my head and threw it into the back of the truck. Squirting some of the cold water over my chest and down my back, I tried to keep the smirk off my face. If she was watching, I was giving her a helluva show. I grabbed the ice towel and headed for the shade. I had to go fix the fence in the few places that Wilson had pointed out, but I needed to cool down a bit first.

Leaning against the tree, I took another swig of water and wrapped the ice towel around my neck. The breeze was nicer when the scorching sun wasn't beating down on you.

"What did you do to Becca Lynn?"

Snapping my head up from its resting place against the tree, I took in the first real sight of Eva I'd had since the night at the lake. Her long brown hair was pulled back into a ponytail. She was wearing a short white cotton sundress and a pair of flip-flops. She was also trying really hard to look stern. She wasn't upset with me. She was just being nosy. I liked that.

"Good morning to you, too, Eva," I replied, unable to keep from smiling.

She tilted her head to one side and continued to force that frown. I'd seen the real thing. This was not the real "angry Eva" face. "Becca Lynn hasn't come around in two days. That isn't normal. Especially since she was so hot after you. So what did you do to her?"

"I believe it's what I didn't do to her." I took a slow swig of my water, but I didn't take my eyes off her as she let my words sink in.

Shifting her feet, she put her hands on her hips. "What does that mean?"

"It means exactly what it sounds like. I didn't do her. I'm guessing that's the problem."

Eva's fake scowl disappeared, and she was frowning. "But I saw you both naked at the . . ." She trailed off, and her eyes grew wider. Two pink splotches covered her cheeks. Eva Brooks had come back to the lake the other night. She'd seen me naked. Yeah, I was going to have to spend a lot of fucking time in the shower now. The image of her sneaking around to see me naked was just hot.

"Did Eva Brooks come back to the lake and get an eyeful?" I teased.

I was sure she'd spin around and run off, but she didn't.

"I didn't mean to see anything. I was coming back to talk to you about . . . I was just . . ." She couldn't say it. I needed her to finish that thought. She was coming to talk to me? Why?

"I was pretty sure you were ready to run me over with your truck that night. Why would you have come back to talk to me?"

Eva twisted her hands nervously. I'd never seen her act nervous before. "It's about Jeremy and me," she began. I waited, hoping she was going to shed some light on their screwed-up relationship.

A movement out of the corner of my eye caught my attention. Grabbing Eva's shoulders, I shoved her behind me and faced down the big-ass cows standing a few feet away from us. They were out of the pasture. How the fuck had they gotten past the fence?

"What are you doing?" Eva squealed, slapping at my back as I pinned her against the tree with my body. I wasn't much of a barrier between her and the cows, but at the moment this was the best idea I had.

"Stop hitting me!" I demanded. "And tell me how the hell I get these big-ass motherfuckers back through the gate."

Eva stopped slapping me only to shove me hard. "Oh, for crying out loud, Cage. They aren't going to charge us." She pushed her way out from behind me and shot me an amused smirk. "They aren't bulls."

Who the fuck cared if they were bulls are not? They were freaking huge.

Eva walked toward them without an ounce of fear and began hollering at them to go on. She stomped her feet, causing them to back up, and then they slowly began to move toward the gate that had been left open. She glanced back at me over her shoulder and rolled her eyes. "They're ferocious beasts, aren't they?"

I was torn between feeling like an idiot and laughing at how damn cute she looked herding cattle.

Once she had the last one back on the other side of the

fence, she closed it and put the lock in place. "Might help if you lock them up next time," she chirped in a playful tone.

"You're enjoying this just a little too much," I replied.

She shrugged and crossed her arms in front of her chest. "I gotta admit, your gallantry at attempting to save me from the big bad mean cows was noble in a moronic sort of way."

"Moronic, huh?" I liked seeing her playful and amused. So far all I'd seen was the uptight version of Eva Brooks.

"You can't be a very good cowhand if you're scared of the cows."

I let out a sigh. "Well, damn, there went my future plans."

What looked like the tugging of a smile appeared on her lips but vanished just as quickly. The playful glint in her eyes disappeared as well. What had I done to put her back in a bad mood? I liked the Eva I'd just gotten a glimpse of, not this sad, snarky one who had reappeared.

"We're not engaged. Jeremy and I are friends. Very good friends."

Confused, I dropped my eyes to the ring on her left hand just to make sure I hadn't imagined seeing it. The diamond was still there, professing to the world that she was an engaged woman. Who the hell was she engaged to? The only guy I'd seen her with was Jeremy.

"You wear that ring for fun?" I asked jokingly, in hopes of getting the fun Eva back, but instead her face fell.

"No. I don't wear it for fun. I'm not engaged to Jeremy. I'm engaged to his brother."

EVA

"I'm engaged to his brother"? Why had I said it like I was still engaged to Josh? He was going to find out the truth. I'd darted away so fast that he couldn't ask me any more questions, but he would ask someone. Not that I thought he was really curious about me, but because he was confused. I didn't want him curious about Josh. I didn't want him to know about everything that had happened.

I wanted him to still look at me with that appreciative, sexy gleam in his eyes. The gleam I would continue to ignore. I liked having someone look at me with something other than sympathy. Once he knew, those sexy smirks and those strip-teases he did outside for my benefit would all end. He'd feel bad for poor Eva.

Until he'd shown up, I hadn't realized that everyone looked at me differently. They were careful with me. Cage didn't look at me like I was breakable. Ten months ago I hadn't been ready for someone to look at me differently. I'd wanted them to remember Josh when they saw me. Now I needed someone, anyone, to just see me. Not the tragedy. Just me.

Cage didn't know my past. He didn't know the pain I'd

suffered. He didn't measure every word he spoke to me, and he didn't hold back punches. He treated me like he did everyone else. With him, I felt normal again. It was about time I felt like a human again.

The screen door slammed behind me, and I jumped.

"Damn, Charles North thinks he can just go on up to my hunting camp whenever he damn well pleases with a bunch of banker friends of his," Daddy grumbled as he walked into the kitchen.

Charles North was my mother's sister's husband. My mother had passed away when I was seven, so I never really got to know her sister or her sister's husband. All I did know was that my dad was not a fan. My aunt Kim only ever called when she wanted something. She acted like Daddy owed her something because my momma was killed in a car accident. Daddy hadn't been driving, but that didn't seem to make a difference to my aunt. She still blamed him.

"What happened?" I asked, reaching into the cabinet to get him a glass.

He took it from my hand and went about pouring himself some lemonade.

"Your aunt Kim called and informed me that Charles would be going fishing up at the camp this weekend. He was bringing friends with him. No one asked me. They just took it upon themselves to make these plans. Well, I told Josiah that he could take Jeremy up to the camp this weekend and they could go fishing. I am not changing that." Daddy shook his head and took a really long swig of the lemonade.

"You going up there?" I asked as he finished his drink and set it on the table in front of him.

"Yeah, got to. I'll head out in the morning. Cage knows what to do out there, and then he will be gone on Sunday. That's his day off. He already told me he has a ride back to the beach for the day."

Cage would be gone all day Sunday? I wouldn't have to worry about him getting too hot outside, so I should be relieved, but I wasn't. I didn't want him to go. I'd be left alone out here all by myself.

"Okay," I managed to reply.

"I'm gonna go into town and get some more barbed wire for the fence. Damn bull keeps tearing up that piece of the fence down by the lake. Guess he wants out to take a swim," Dad grumbled as he headed for the door.

I waited until I heard Daddy's truck leave the drive before heading outside. I wasn't sure exactly what I was doing. It was a spur-of-the-moment decision. Cage had walked into the barn just a few minutes ago. I'd watched him from the kitchen window.

I headed to the barn.

Opening the door, I stepped inside. I had to squint to see

clearly. The only light streaming into the barn was from the cracks in the roof, so it was dark compared to the bright sunshine outside. The familiar smell of hay and wood hit me as I turned to see if Cage was still in here. I'd had my back to the window when Daddy had been in the kitchen, so it was possible he'd left and I'd missed him.

"Looking for something?" Cage asked from behind me.

I turned around to face him and almost swallowed my tongue when my eyes met his naked chest. I'd admired it from afar but never up close. It was better up close.

"An engaged lady shouldn't be looking at another man like she wants to take a lick." The teasing tone in his voice told me he didn't really mind my gawking at him at all. He was enjoying it.

"Who said I wanted to take a lick?" I replied, surprised at my own response. Was that flirting I had just done? I wasn't sure I'd ever flirted.

Cage ran a hand through his hair and let out a short, deep laugh. "Maybe we ought to change the subject." Cage was nervous. Had my comment just made him nervous?

"You brought up the licking, Cage, not me." I waited to see how he'd react this time.

"Yeah, I guess I did," he drawled, and took a step toward me. Okay, so maybe I hadn't made him nervous. Guys like Cage probably didn't get nervous. "If you really want to talk about licking, I'll happily oblige."

Oh my. Now I was nervous. Cage reached out and took my left hand in his. The warmth from his callused palm made my entire body tingle. "Only problem with talking about licking with you is that it gives me ideas. I start thinking about things I shouldn't be thinking about. Things that will only torment me 'cause I'll never know just how sweet you taste. I may be a lot of things, Eva, may even be a few of them names you called me, but I'm not gonna touch what belongs to another man."

I opened my mouth to say something but stopped when Cage lifted my left hand to his mouth and kissed my ring finger. Then his tongue darted out and just barely skimmed the top of my hand. He grinned wickedly.

At some point, I'd stopped breathing. When my lungs started burning, I took a deep breath, and Cage let my hand fall back to my side. "Sorry, I had to take one small taste." Then he winked at me and turned toward the door.

I stood silently as he walked back outside into the summer heat.

Chapter Six

CAGE

I drove as far away from that damn barn as I could get. When the lake came into view, I pulled over and jumped out of the truck. Then I started for the water. I needed to cool the fuck off. I'd wanted to stop Eva from any more of her flirty little remarks, and damned if I hadn't just screwed myself. Stupid. Stupid. Stupid.

I started unbuttoning my jeans.

"Hey, if you plan on stripping, give me time to get gone first." I spun around to see Jeremy walking over from his side of the fence. Not exactly who I wanted to see at the moment. My head was all kinds of screwed up over his future sister-in-law.

"It's hot," I replied. The annoyance in my tone was unavoidable. I was pissed. I had no reason to be, but I was. Why hadn't I just banged Becca Lynn and taken the edge off? It would have given me physical relief and pissed Eva off. If she went back to hating me, then she'd stop hunting me down and saying shit she had no business saying.

"Yeah, it is. We don't get much of that gulf breeze out here like y'all do down on the coast."

I wasn't in the mood to talk about the weather.

"You working?" I asked before I told him to run the fuck off so I could strip.

"Nah, I'm done. Going fishing with my dad this weekend. Thought I'd come down here and check out the fence line before we headed out."

Just his dad? He'd never mentioned his brother. Not once. That was odd.

"Your brother going too?"

Jeremy's easy smile vanished. "Uh, no."

"He not live around here? I've never seen him at Eva's."

Jeremy stuck his hands in the front pockets of his jeans, and his frown deepened. "What do you know about my brother?"

"Nothing except that he's engaged to Eva." What was the deal here? Why the weirdness about his brother? It was a simple question.

"Eva tell you that?" Jeremy asked, still frowning.

"Yeah."

Jeremy let out a deep sigh and shook his head. Something was way off here.

"I really shouldn't tell you this because it's Eva's story to tell. Still, you at least need to know the truth. Eva was engaged to my brother."

They broke it off? Except she was still wearing the ring. Was she mentally off? Was that what I was missing here?

"Cage, my brother is dead."

That had not been what I was expecting. I had almost been convinced Eva was a little unstable. I sure wasn't expecting to hear she was wearing the ring her dead fiancé had given her.

"He was in the army. About eighteen months ago, a bomb near Baghdad. Him along with four other soldiers. He'd proposed to Eva on his last leave."

Well, shit. "She still wears the ring," I said, trying to wrap my head around this.

"Yeah, she does. They grew up together. We all did. He was my twin. But he and Eva were inseparable. They were so alike."

I didn't have a response for this. What could I say? I was sorry? That seemed too shallow. The guy had lost his brother. Eva had lost her fiancé. Sorry wasn't exactly deep enough.

"Do me a favor and don't tell her I told you. She isn't over it. As you can see, she still wears the ring, and don't get me started on that badass Jeep she has and won't drive." He stopped, and the concern in his eyes was clear. He didn't want Eva upset.

"I won't tell her I know," I assured him.

"Thanks, man." He was starting to turn and walk away when

he stopped and looked back at me. "Remember this the next time she acts like a complete bitch. She hasn't given you a fair chance, but I've decided it's because she's attracted to you and it scares her. I doubt she ever gives you a break. Just ignore it."

She'd started to give me some sort of break in the barn earlier. Sure as hell wish I'd stayed around to find out what it was now that I knew this. I'd run because I was real close to kissing her pretty little lips. Her being engaged had been a red flag. Then there was my scholarship I had to think about. But truth be told, if Eva pushed hard enough, I'd break.

"Hey, Jeremy," I called out, and he stopped again. "She ever smile?"

I'd been waiting to see her smile. I thought maybe it was just me she didn't smile around. After hearing this, I wondered if she ever smiled anymore.

"Haven't seen her smile since the day before we got the call about Josh. It was the weekend, and I'd decided to surprise everyone by coming home from Vanderbilt. I remember walking in the door to the kitchen, and Eva was sitting at the table with Momma looking over wedding magazines. Both of them squealed and jumped up to hug me. We got the call the next morning."

My chest hurt. I wasn't a real emotional guy. I'd had a shit life for the most part. Even so, the picture he'd just painted of a happy Eva with her life ahead of her, then having it snatched away . . . hurt me.

"What's her smile like?" I asked.

Jeremy looked wistful for a moment. Then replied, "Incredible."

EVA

Daddy was gone for the weekend, and Cage would be gone tomorrow. Even Jeremy wouldn't be around. I thought about calling Becca Lynn, but then I wasn't sure I wanted her around here just yet. Whatever had happened with her and Cage hadn't been something she'd enjoyed, because she hadn't called me or come by.

I wrapped Saran wrap around the two turkey-and-swiss subs I'd made Cage for dinner. I hadn't cooked anything, but Cage would need to eat. I reached under the counter and pulled out a sports bottle. He had to be tired of water. I filled it up with the rest of the lemonade I'd made for Daddy.

Unable to resist, I left both items sitting on the counter and went to the mirror in the hallway to check my hair and face. I wasn't going to think too hard about why I wanted to look attractive for Cage. If I did think about it, the answer would more than likely bother me.

Once I was sure I looked good enough, I went back to the kitchen and picked up the plate of food, grabbed a bag of chips and the lemonade, and then headed to the barn.

The sun was setting, and it was later than I normally brought his dinner out. Most of the time, I managed to get here before he finished working and left it on the table by his bed. But tonight I wanted to see him. I wanted him to touch my hand again and make my body tingle. It had been so long since a single touch had made me feel alive. It was exciting. I missed excitement.

I opened the barn door. Looking to the right, I saw the door to his room closed. The only air-conditioner in the barn was the small window unit in the back room. Keeping the door closed was the only way for him to keep the room cold, so he always kept it closed. I typically didn't have to question whether he was in there or not because I knew he wasn't. But I hadn't seen him come inside, so all I had to go on was the fact that the truck was parked outside.

With a tight grip on the plate in my hand, I made my way to his door. I started to knock and decided to lean forward and listen first. Maybe he was in the shower or on the phone. I pressed my ear to the warm wood. I couldn't hear anything. I bent down and set the sports bottle at my feet, then cupped my hand to my ear to see if it made hearing through the wood easier.

"What's going on in there? Can't be a whole lot. It's too damn small." Cage's amused voice startled me, and I fumbled with the plate I was holding with one hand.

"Whoa, girl. Don't drop my dinner." He laughed. Then he reached out and took the plate from my hands.

I'd been caught trying to eavesdrop on him. This could not be more embarrassing. Crawling under my bed and not coming out for a week sounded appealing right about now.

"Before you kick it over, can I have that bottle down there?" He pointed to the lemonade I had set down so I could be more efficient in my eavesdropping. I bent back down and picked it up. Maybe I could hand it to him and then run out of here without having to actually make eye contact. I held out the sports bottle but kept my eyes diverted from his. I could feel the amusement on his face. I didn't have to see it.

"Ah, come on now, Eva. You can't not look at me. You had no problem listening in at my door. Who knows what you could have heard if I'd been in there?"

He was teasing me, and he had every right to. I couldn't keep the small bubble of laughter down. Lifting my eyes, I met his gaze. "I can't believe you caught me," I replied honestly.

I expected him to crack another joke, but his face was no longer amused. He appeared to be studying me closely. A pleased smile formed on his lips, and he held up the plate of subs. "There are two subs here. You gonna eat with me?"

Oh. Wow. Um. No. I was starting to shake my head when he leaned forward, causing me to shiver from the warmth of his skin.

"And why not?" he asked in a husky whisper as the door behind me started to open.

"I already ate," I blurted out.

"Then keep me company while I eat," he replied, leaning back away from me now that he had the door behind me opened. "Go on in, Eva. It's nice and cool."

This was when I should've politely refused and gone back to the house. Except I didn't. I turned and walked into the small room that Cage occupied.

Like all the other times I'd been in here to leave his meals, the bed was a mess. He never made it up. There was also a pile of dirty clothes in the corner. The only neat habit the boy had was that he hung up his bath towel every night on the back of the door. I remembered that I'd only left him one towel and one washcloth when I'd prepared the room for him. Was he having to use the same washcloth? I felt guilty for being such a judgmental brat earlier this week. He'd worked hard all week. He deserved a clean washcloth and towel every night.

Cage walked around me since I'd stopped in the middle of the room, and he went to take a seat on his unmade bed. He began unwrapping the plate of subs like he hadn't been fed in days. Glancing at the clock on the wall over his bed, I saw it was after eight. It had been over six hours since I'd brought him out fresh water and a slice of Mrs. Mabel's lemon pound cake. Another stirring of guilt at how I'd been treating him churned in my stomach.

"If that isn't enough, I can go make another one or two," I offered as he took a large bite out of the sub.

He grinned as he chewed, then took a long swig of the lemonade. "This is great. Thanks. I was starving. And the lemon cake thing the invisible fairy brought me earlier was fu— amazing too."

What? "Invisible fairy?" I asked, confused.

Cage looked so sincere. "You know, the fairy who magically brings me water and ice rags when my back is turned."

He wanted to be a smart guy, huh? Well, fine, two could play that game.

"Oh, that fairy. Yeah, she has an aversion to cocky guys who think they have the world at their fingertips."

Cage set the sub in his hand back down and narrowed his eyes. "Is that so? Hmm . . . and here I was hoping she was going to finally appear one day and give me a nice diversion from work."

"Highly doubtful," I replied, unable to keep from grinning.

"Well, day-um. I'll have to come up with something other than my sexy topless fairy fantasy the next time I need a break."

Oh dear God, did he mean . . . ? "You are sick," I said through my appalled laughter.

"Who, me? You were the one listening at my door. What was it you were hoping to hear, Eva? If I'd known you were coming in hope of a show, I could have been more prepared."

Chapter Seven

CAGE

Damn if her smile wasn't fucking gorgeous. Not to mention that laugh—I wanted to soak it in and keep it for later. Just knowing it was me making her smile made everything else seem less important.

"I was just making sure you weren't in the shower or on the phone," she explained.

Sure. That's what she'd been doing when I'd stood there in the shadows of the barn and watched her try so hard to hear something through the door. It had taken all my willpower not to burst into laughter.

"Were you gonna come on in if I was in the shower? You've already seen my naked ass."

Eva blushed again. She must have gotten a pretty damn good view.

"I need to get back to the house," she said, and started to move back to the door.

"Please don't go. I won't tease you anymore, I promise." I wanted her to stay. I wanted to get to know her, and I wanted her to trust me enough to tell me the truth about that ring on her finger.

I could see the indecision on her face. That was a good sign. Some part of her wanted to stay here. "Aren't you exhausted?" she asked.

I was extremely exhausted, but I wasn't ready to give her up just yet. "Not really. Just lonely. All my friends are an hour away. I need a friend here."

Eva stepped over and sat down on the very end of the bed. She was staying.

"Are you asking me to be your friend, Cage York?"

Not exactly. But for now friends would do. "I guess I am."

"Why would you want me for a friend? I've been nothing but mean to you since you got here."

Because you fascinate me. She wasn't ready to hear that yet. "I'm guessing you control whether or not my sheets get washed. I figured if we were buds, then that would happen more often."

"No, you control whether or not your sheets get washed. You know where the soap and water are located," she shot back at me.

She really was a snot when she wanted to be. "Well, in that

case, I'm going to have to get a female out here who likes me enough to help me out."

I could see by her expression that she thought I was joking. I wasn't. I really intended to call Low and get her to stop by my place and get me some clean sheets and a couple washcloths and towels. I also needed some shampoo and soap. I was tired of washing my hair and body with the dish detergent that I'd found under the sink by the feed station.

"Good luck with that," she chirped.

I finished off my second sub and opened the bag of chips before leaning back against the wall and propping my legs up on the bed. "You might be surprised what I can wrangle up."

Eva rolled her eyes and shifted so she was facing me. "Your ego knows no bounds, does it?"

I popped a chip into my mouth and chewed slowly, enjoying the grease. Eva studied me as I chewed. Her eyes dropped down to my neck. What was she looking at my neck for? Then the tip of her pink tongue darted out and licked her bottom lip. Well, damn.

I was only so strong. I set the bag of chips on the bed and swung my legs back down to the floor. Her eyes widened in surprise and lifted back up to meet my gaze. I stopped in front of her and reached down to take her hand and pull her up until she was standing. I gently tugged her up against me, and then before she had time to think or refuse, I covered her plump red lips with mine.

She was stiff in my arms for only a moment. Her lips loosened up, and she began eagerly kissing me back. I took a small nip on her upper lip, then trailed small kisses across her bottom lip and licked each warm corner. When a sigh escaped her mouth, I took complete advantage and slipped my tongue inside the dark warmth of her mouth. It was sweeter than I'd imagined. She tasted like lemonade and sunshine. Her tongue began to join in on the exploring, and for the first time in my life my knees went a little weak.

I slipped both my hands around her waist and settled them on her hips. I wanted to explore her body the way I was getting to explore the silky confines of her mouth, but I wasn't sure she was ready for more. Slowly her hands slid up my chest over the soft cotton of my T-shirt. She ran the pads of her thumbs over my nipples, and I gripped her waist tighter, forcing myself to keep my hands in a safe area. Fuck, when had I ever kept my damn hands in a safe area? How the hell did I know what a safe area was?

The soft moan that escaped her mouth was my undoing. My hands slipped up her ribs and cupped both of her boobs. The hard pebbles of her nipples pressed against the fabric of her bra and shirt. That wasn't enough. I needed more. I reached down and began lifting up the hem of her shirt while eagerly dropping kisses along her jawline and nibbling on her ear.

"Cage, no."

I froze. Motherfucker.

I let the hem of her top fall back down over her bare stomach, and I stepped away from her. The smell of her skin and taste of her lips clung to me. Closing my eyes, I took a deep breath. That wasn't enough. I needed more distance.

"Then go," I replied in a ragged breath.

"I'm sorry—"

"Don't be sorry. No reason to be. I just need you to go," I managed to choke out.

Once the door closed behind her, I turned and opened the shower curtain, then reached in and turned the water on cold.

EVA

Sleep had eluded me all night. Every time I closed my eyes, all I could see was that kiss. Then it would switch and I would be kissing Josh. It wasn't as passionate and insane. It hadn't felt as wickedly delicious. Then the guilt would set in. Josh had been perfect and good. Josh had loved me and only me. Cage was nothing good and far from perfect except for his outer appearance. Cage just liked women. He didn't love me. He'd never love anyone. I had to be the worst kind of person to even admit that Cage York's kiss had been the most mind-blowing thing I'd ever experienced, when Josh had kissed me many times. He'd held me in his arms and danced with me in the moonlight. How could I think Cage's meaningless kiss felt better than even a moment in Josh's presence?

Throwing the covers back, I gave up trying to sleep. It was morning, anyway. I grabbed a pair of shorts and a short-sleeved top from my closet and headed down the hall for my bathroom. Cage would be leaving today. Should I let him go without saying anything to him about my abrupt departure last night, or should I go ahead and talk this out now? I decided I'd get it over with instead of thinking about it all day long.

Once I was clean and dressed, I headed outside. A silver hatchback was parked in the driveway. Cage's ride must be here. I made my way down to the barn and noticed that the truck he used for work was gone. Had he gone to do something before he left?

The barn door swung open, and out walked a curvy redhead. She was carrying what looked like bedsheets and a towel. When her eyes met mine, she smiled and began walking toward me. The short skirt she was wearing showcased a pair of really amazing legs. I hated her. Then she got close enough for me to see the crystal-green color of her eyes, and I really, really hated her. Who was she, and why was she in my barn?

"Hey, I'm Willow, a friend of Cage's. I brought him clean sheets and some towels and washcloths. I thought I'd take these home with me today and wash them. He can bring them back this evening. That way he can have an extra set."

He hadn't been kidding about getting some help. But

I'd been kidding about not washing his sheets. I was going to change them today and make sure he had enough towels and washcloths for the week. It irritated me that this girl had beat me to it. Figures Cage would have gorgeous females at his beck and call. Who was I kidding? If I turned him down, he just had a line of women waiting for their chance. The fact that I'd left him last night was probably off his radar this morning. All we'd done was kiss. I'd lost sleep over it, and Cage had been busy calling his "friend" to get her to bring him clean sheets and towels. *Ugh!*

"I'll take the sheets. I don't mind washing them. I was going to wash them today while he was gone." The annoyed tone in my voice didn't go unnoticed.

A worried frown crinkled her forehead. "Oh. I'm sorry. I guess he didn't want to bother y'all. He called me and asked if I'd mind bringing him some things he needed, and he mentioned the sheets. I figured while I waited on him to feed the cows I could go ahead and change the sheets."

She was too attractive to be on some guy's speed dial to jump when he said jump. Did the girl not feel any self-worth? Her daddy should have taught her that she was more than some man's doormat. Cage's face and body probably got girls to do anything he wanted. Not me. I would not become another one of his many fans. I had pride. "I'm sure Cage could have managed on his own," I clipped out, and took the sheets and one dirty towel and washcloth from her arms.

Willow laughed. "You would think. Unfortunately, he's grown accustomed to females taking care of him. This is roughing it for him. Granted, he needed this wake-up call. Anything to get him to stop drinking and driving."

She sure knew a lot about him. Did he keep this one around on a regular basis? I didn't peg him for a guy to keep one girl close. Or maybe she just knew the rules and was okay with them. Again, her daddy should have taught her better.

The farm truck rattled as it came rolling to a stop out beside the barn. Willow flashed a smile at me, then waved to Cage as he climbed out. Why was he shirtless already? It was eight in the morning. All he'd done was feed the cows.

"Low, you bring the stuff?" he called out as he sauntered toward us.

"Yes, and I put it all away in your room for you. Even made up your bed. It's nice and clean."

"What about a shirt?"

Willow nodded. "Yep, it's on your bed."

He stopped in front of Willow and pulled her into a bear hug, then buried his head in the curve of her neck. She patted his back and laughed at something he mumbled against her head full of hair. I wasn't really up for watching the two of them make out, so I started to turn and walk back to the house with my arms full of dirty laundry.

"Eva, wait. Did you meet Low?"

Great, he wanted to introduce us. What was I supposed to say to her? I'd been the one kissing him last night, and now she'd be the one kissing and probably screwing him today.

"Yeah, I did," I replied as coldly as possible.

Cage frowned and looked down at Low as if she had the answer to why I was annoyed. "Okay, well, I'm heading out. I'll see you tonight. I got the cows fed. Everything should be fine."

With one curt nod, I turned and walked as quickly as I could to the house. I had to go inside and get a grip. All the guy had done was kiss me. Why was I acting like he and I had something more? We had nothing. He was as unavailable to me as a guy could get.

Throwing the sheets into the washing machine, I scowled at the cotton bedclothes as if it were their fault. Stupid redhead had to come. She'd changed his sheets for him and brought him more towels and washcloths because I'd neglected to give him sufficient supplies. Great job, Eva.

Chapter Eight

CAGE

"What the hell did you do to Eva?" I asked as I climbed into the passenger seat of Low's Volvo. I'd been hoping to smooth things over with Eva before I left today, but she'd been prickly, so I'd kept my distance. No reason to ruffle her feathers in front of Low.

"So you noticed that too? I thought I was just being paranoid. I've got no idea what I did to set her off, but I got the distinct impression that she did not like me bringing you clean sheets and making up your bed for you." Low shot me a warning glare. "You haven't done anything with her, have you, Cage? She's engaged."

I let my head fall back on the headrest and sighed. I almost felt like I was betraying Eva if I told Low the truth. But, hell, I had to tell someone. Low was the best friend I had, and she was a female. Maybe she could help me figure this out.

"She isn't exactly engaged," I began.

"*Yes*, she is. I saw the diamond on her left hand."

"Yeah, I know that, but the guy who put that ring on her finger was killed in Baghdad eighteen months ago."

Low's sharp intake of breath was followed by an "Ohmygod."

"The guy I thought she was engaged to turned out to be her fiancé's twin. They're just good friends."

"But she still wears the ring," Low whispered. "How incredibly sad. When did she tell you this?"

I wondered if she ever would tell me this. Last night, even though it had sent her running, that had been one helluva kiss. Even before the kiss, we'd talked and she'd laughed. Not just smiled, but she'd laughed.

"She didn't. Jeremy did."

"Jeremy? He's her fiancé's twin?"

"Yeah."

"That just breaks my heart, Cage."

The ache that throbbed in my chest when I let myself think about Eva's pain returned. "She isn't the bitch she appears to be. She's really a lot of fun if you can get past her walls of steel."

Low cleared her throat and shifted in her seat. "Do I take it this means you got past those steel walls?"

"A little. I made her smile and laugh. Jeremy said she hadn't smiled since the day before Josh's death."

Low reached over and patted my knee. "If she's smart enough to let you in, the real you, not the one you share with the females whose panties you just want to get in, then she's a smart woman."

"It ain't about her panties," I replied, reaching down to squeeze her hand.

"No, Cage, with you, it is about her panties at least a little bit. But I think that maybe this time you want more."

Did I want more? Was it just because she was so damn hard to get? Or did I really want more?

"Yeah, you're right. The panties are always on my priority list."

Low shook her head and laughed. "I've missed you this week. Live Bay isn't the same without you there with us. I even think Preston may have shed a tear when you weren't there to sing Kid Rock's part of 'Picture' when they played it over the speakers while the band was on break."

"Did he sing Sheryl Crow's and Kid's parts all by himself?" I asked.

"Yes, unfortunately, he did. Standing on the table with some random stranger's brush in his hands as his microphone."

"Bet that was funny as shit," I replied.

"Or nightmare worthy. Depends on how you look at it."

The one-hour trip with Marcus was easier this time. He wasn't pissed off the entire trip. Probably because Low was so damn happy I hadn't been fired yet. After he dropped me off, I thought of stopping by the house and talking to Eva. Her dad's truck was still gone. But she probably wouldn't be real thrilled about me showing up at her door at nine o'clock at night. Might just need to wait until she came to me.

Before I could get to the far end of the house, I heard the gravel crunch in the driveway as a car pulled in. Turning around, I checked to make sure it was Wilson. I didn't want just anyone showing up, with Eva alone in the house.

The passenger door of Jeremy's truck swung open, and Eva jumped out.

"Cageisback!" she slurred happily. Her hand was gripping the door to steady herself.

"Eva! Dammit, I told you to wait on me. You're gonna fall down on the gravel and get hurt." Jeremy ran around the front of the truck and quickly wrapped his arm around Eva's waist.

"She's drunk?" I asked in amazement as I walked back toward the driveway, still not sure I was seeing what it looked like.

"Hammered is more like it. She went out to the damn honky-tonk with Becca Lynn. I got a call from Nelly, the owner, about an hour ago. She said I needed to come get Eva. Becca Lynn was passed out on top of the bar. She'd already called Becca's daddy."

"Itwasfun," Eva said with a sloppy grin, and stepped out of Jeremy's arms and into my chest. I wrapped my arms around her quickly to keep her from face-planting on the gravel.

"Yeah, looks like you had yourself a good ol' time," I replied as she slipped her arms up my chest and clasped her hands tightly behind my neck.

"Youshouldcometoo."

Nodding, I lifted my gaze from her adorably drunk expression to look at Jeremy. He was standing behind her, waiting on her next move.

"We need to get her to bed. Her daddy ain't coming home till tomorrow. He's still got a bunch of people up at his hunting camp."

"Should she be left alone in the house like this?" I asked as she leaned heavily on me.

"Probably not." Jeremy rubbed his hand through his hair and glanced back at his truck. He had other plans. I could tell he was trying real hard to figure out the right thing to do.

"I gotta get some stuff packed up tonight and head out early in the morning to check on an apartment I'm looking at moving into with my cousin in the fall. You think you could watch her?"

So Jeremy was getting ready to move on with his life. Had he told Eva yet? Was that why she was completely wasted?

"I got her. You go on. We'll be fine."

The indecision on his face as he studied the back of Eva's head had me thinking he might end up staying to watch her after all. I understood that kind of protective streak. I had it with Low. Eva rested her head against my chest.

"You good with that, Eva?" Jeremy asked.

"Mmmmmm-hmmmm," she replied, then began sniffing my shirt.

Jeremy shook his head then looked back up at me. "She's dealing with life. It's moving on without Josh, and she's just now realizing it. Be good to her."

"Of course," I replied, and dropped a kiss to the top of her cigarette-scented hair. Not something I would have expected to smell on Eva Brooks.

Jeremy studied me a moment, and then with a quick nod he turned and headed back to his truck. I waited until he was pulling out of the drive before moving Eva.

"I need to get you to your bed, sweetheart. Do you want me to pick you up, or do you want to walk? Or do you need to puke?"

Eva giggled against my chest and tilted her head back to smile sleepily at me. "Takemetoyourbed," she slurred.

"Now, that's a bad idea, beautiful. You see, when you're sober, my bed is the last place you wanna be."

She shook her head and, standing on her tiptoes, pressed a tequila-tasting kiss to my mouth.

"I wanna sleep in your bed, puhlease." She managed not to run her words together this time.

How was I supposed to tell her no when she was all sweet and playful? She was drunk off her ass, but she was a nice drunk.

"Just sleep?" I asked.

"Jussleep."

I bent down and slipped my arm under her knees, then cradled her against my chest and carried her to the barn. This was probably not my most intelligent moment, but I wasn't about to give up what could be my only chance at sleeping all night with Eva Brooks in my arms.

EVA

"Don't you go to sleep yet. You need to drink this water and take the aspirin first." Cage's voice was even sexy when he was being all bossy.

I giggled and stared up at him as he stood hovering over me. His bed was nice and soft, and I really just wanted to close my eyes. How was a girl supposed to turn down orders from a guy who looked like that? I stuck my arm up in the air. "Pull me up," I told him. Cage grinned and reached for my hand, which was unfortunately numb, so I didn't get the complete enjoyment from his touch.

Once he had me sitting up on the edge of the bed, he squatted down in front of me until we were at eye level. The glass of water he'd run up to the house to get was in one hand and the white chalky pills I hated were in the other.

"Can I just drink the water?" I asked, scowling at the pills. I hated swallowing pills. I did it if I absolutely had to, but I hated the taste they left in my mouth and the way they felt going down.

"If you don't take the aspirin, you're going to have one helluva hangover in the morning. Drink this whole glass of water and take the pills."

His voice was all deep and hypnotic. I wondered if he'd talk to me while I fell asleep. I'd have to ask him that. First I needed to drink the water.

"I hate swallowing pills," I grumbled, reaching for the glass.

Cage's smile reappeared, and he reached up and tucked a lock of my hair behind my ear. I'd tried to tuck that hair behind my ear earlier, but I couldn't get my hand to cooperate. I kept missing my ear.

"You can do it. I'm right here if you need me. I'll even hold your hand. Just please, Eva, swallow the pills."

His eyes were too ridiculously pretty to belong to a guy. Especially a guy with abs like his and back muscles . . . Oh, I liked those back muscles.

"It's not fair that your eyelashes are so long and curly. Girls spend a lot of time and money trying to get eyelashes like yours."

Cage laughed and reached up and ran his thumb under my left eye. "Yeah, well, my eyelashes have got nothing on your eyes. They're fucking incredible."

Oh. Wow.

"I wish I hadn't run off last night," I admitted as he continued to caress my cheekbone, then my jawline.

"It was a good thing you did. I was close to losing my control." His voice had dropped to a husky whisper that made me shiver.

"Maybe I wanted you to lose control."

Cage's grin returned. "You're drunk, Eva. I can assure you that the sober Eva doesn't want me to lose control. She wants me to keep my distance."

Was that true? No, it wasn't. The sober Eva was just so determined to live by her own set of rules.

"Drink the water." Cage nudged the glass toward my mouth.

I took a small sip, and the taste of cold water on my tongue was refreshing. I hadn't realized how dry my mouth was. I took several longer swallows before Cage reached up and took the glass from me.

"Now take the aspirin," he ordered, holding the pills up for me. Obediently I opened my mouth, and he placed them on my tongue. He brought the water back up to my lips, and I swallowed the pills with ease. I didn't even taste them. Maybe I should just get drunk every time I got sick and needed to take pills. Maybe I just needed Cage to give them to me.

"Good girl," he said as I finished the rest of the water. "Now lie back down, but scoot your cute little ass over against the wall. I have to fit in this bed too."

Looking up at his wide shoulders and long legs, I began wondering if that was going to be possible. I really didn't want to sleep in the house tonight. I wanted to be with Cage. But was I making it hard for him to get good rest?

"I'll make it work. I happen to know exactly how to sleep in bed with a girl comfortably," he assured me. I scooted over until my whole left side was touching the wall. "Now roll over on your side, facing the wall."

I did as he instructed. Then the bed dipped down with his weight and he slid in behind me. One warm arm wrapped around my stomach as he tucked himself against my back. This was nice. Really nice.

"Cage?"

"Yeah?"

I wanted to feel close to him. I didn't want the lies between us anymore. But the thought of saying Josh's name while drunk and snuggled up against Cage seemed wrong. I couldn't do it. So, instead, I closed my eyes.

Chapter Nine

CAGE

After a week of waking up with the sun, my eyes easily popped open before the sunrise was complete. Eva was making some soft purring sound in her sleep. Her legs had gotten all tangled up with mine at some point last night.

The smooth silk of her skin sliding against my calves was hard to resist. But I'd managed. I hadn't been a complete angel, though. I couldn't help myself. When she'd grabbed my arm with her hand and pulled it up closer around her, my hand had been left to palm her left boob. So yeah, I'd copped a feel. But damn, I'm a man. They were real nice, too. Soft but firm, and her nipple had been nice and hard even in her sleep.

The erection I had pressed into her ass probably wasn't going to go over real well when sober Eva woke up. As much as

I hated to, I eased my arm from around her and untangled my legs from hers. As quietly as I could, I slipped out of bed. Grabbing a pair of jeans, a work shirt, and my boots, I left the room to go get dressed. I didn't want to wake her. She really needed to sleep that shit off. I'd be willing to bet that was her first drunken experience. She'd been so damn cute. If only sober Eva liked me as much as drunk Eva did. With a sigh, I pulled on my jeans and laced up my boots. It was time to get back to the cows.

Stepping out into the morning sun, I wasn't surprised to see Jeremy there. I wondered if he'd even gotten any sleep, worrying about leaving Eva with me. I had to question his common sense a little. I would've never left Low with a guy like me while she was drunk and not thinking clearly.

Jeremy was pacing back and forth in front of the barn door with a worried frown. His hair looked like either he'd forgot to brush it or he'd been running his hands through it so many times that he'd messed it up good.

"Thought you had to leave early this morning," I said in greeting.

Jeremy stopped pacing and closed the distance between us. He almost looked brave enough to take me on. "Dude, please tell me you didn't—"

"I just gave her aspirin and some water and slept beside her."

"She okay? Did you do anything to her? Is she sick? *Dammit,* I shouldn't have left her. Josh would be furious with me. She

87

was vulnerable, and I just left. I can't just leave." He stopped his tirade and starting pacing again.

"She's fine. I took care of her. She's nice and safe. No harm done."

Jeremy shook his head and kept pacing. "No. No, she isn't okay. She ain't ever gonna be okay. I've been waiting for her to be okay for eighteen months. I know Josh would want me to stay and look out for her. For a year and a half I've been doing what I know he'd have wanted. I gave up my scholarship to Vandy. I lost a semester of school. I went to this dumbass cowpoke community college just so I could stay near her. But I can't keep doing this. I want to live again. I will miss Josh for the rest of my life, but I don't want to keep mourning him." He stopped and put his hands on his hips. His eyes looked glassy, like he was trying to hold back tears. "I can't stop my life for her anymore. But I'm afraid that if no one is here to catch her when she falls, like last night at that damn bar, then she will crash and burn. I'd never be able to forgive myself if something happened to her. She always had Josh. He was her best friend, her protector, and he made her feel complete. But I'm not Josh."

I closed the barn door firmly behind me after checking to see if the bedroom door was still closed. I didn't want Eva hearing this. I understood that Jeremy needed to let this out, but Eva didn't need to be so fucking close when he did.

"Why don't we go somewhere else and talk about this?" I suggested, walking away from the barn and closer to the house.

"You're right. Sorry. Damn, she's still asleep, isn't she?"

I nodded and led him to the front porch, where I had a view of the barn door but we were far enough away that I knew she wouldn't be able to hear us.

Jeremy walked up the steps and ran his hands through his hair again. He even pulled the ends a little as if he were trying to inflict pain on himself.

"I just need to do this," he said. "I need to go to Louisiana and get everything set up for the fall. But every time I think about coming home and telling Eva that I'm leaving in August to go away to school, I feel like I'm gonna vomit."

Poor guy was beating himself up. He was right, though—he couldn't keep putting his life on hold for Eva. She wasn't his responsibility. Just because she'd been his brother's didn't make her his now that his brother was gone. Why hadn't someone told him this before now?

"I've got a best friend who also happens to be a female. I understand what you're feeling. I know that if Low needed me, I'd be there. I'd drop the world for her, but there were times in our lives that I wished I didn't have that responsibility. Difference is, Eva wasn't your best friend. She was your brother's. This isn't about Eva. This is about you wanting to fulfill what you believe your brother's last wishes would have been. In my opinion, you have. I didn't know the dude, but I think you've done your job. I don't think he ever wanted you to give up your life for Eva."

Jeremy sank down onto the old wooden rocker that I'd often seen Eva sitting in while drinking a glass of tea and staring off into space. "You saw her last night. What if that happens when I'm gone?"

Hell, I wasn't a damn psychiatrist. What did he expect from me? He was asking for wisdom from the guy who was working at a farm all summer because of a DUI.

"She's a big girl. She'll be okay. She has her daddy here watching over her, and she has other friends."

Jeremy rubbed the back of his neck nervously. "What about you? While you're here, does she have you?"

Me? What the fuck kind of question was that? She didn't want me. At times I was pretty damn sure she hated me. But, yeah, if she needed me, I knew without question I'd be there. She'd gotten under my skin.

"Yeah, she has me. As long as I'm here, I'll be available if she needs me. Even when she doesn't want me."

Jeremy chuckled and stood up. "She wants you. She just doesn't want to want you. Or at least, that is what she said in my truck last night."

She told Jeremy she didn't want to want me. I liked that. I could work with that. "Drunk Eva was something else," I replied.

Jeremy walked over to the steps and held out his hand. I stared down at it and realized he wanted to shake my hand. I clasped it, and he shook it one good time before letting go. "Take care of her for me."

I nodded. "Will do."

EVA

I couldn't remember what all I'd said to Cage while I was drunk. All I knew was he'd been sweet, and I'd slept in his bed smelling like tequila and an ashtray. While he'd been out working this morning, I'd changed his sheets and made up his bed. I hated for him to sleep on sheets all week that smelled like the inside of a bar.

That was the only contact I'd had with him. I was avoiding him. I was sure he knew that too. I couldn't help but feel guilty about not taking him water and ice towels, but I couldn't bring myself to face him just yet. Had I snored? God, I had probably snored. I didn't even know if I snored. Plus, my breath had to have been atrocious. He'd still let me sleep in his bed with him. How could one girl manage to make such a fool of herself so easily? I really should write a book on how to make an ass of yourself.

Cage hadn't come looking for me today either. He was probably worried I'd think more of what happened than he did. I bet that stupid gorgeous redhead never came to his bed a blubbering idiot and stinking of cigarettes. She just didn't look the type.

I'd run out of things to do in town, and none of the movies playing at the theater had looked appealing. All that was left to do was hide out in the house.

Several vehicles pulled into the driveway, from the sound of all the gravel. I went over to peek outside and see what was going on. It was truckloads of guys. Lots of guys. What in the world? I hurried down the steps and out to the front porch.

Loud insults were being thrown around, along with a whole lot of male laughter and lewd comments. Cage jumped over the fence, and a huge grin broke out on his face as the herd of guys made their way down to the barn.

They were his friends. That much was clear. He fist bumped a few and with his cocky smirk made some comments that I knew were probably something naughty.

"You stay in the house for the next couple of hours," Daddy said as he walked up the steps of the porch with a frown.

"Who are they?" I asked, surprised Cage had let a bunch of guys come see him here.

"It's your uncle Mack's baseball team. He sent them here to have a little bonding time with the boy. He don't want him to get his mind off the goal. I told him it'd be okay for a few hours. They're supposed to take him into town for something to eat and bring him back."

"Can I sit on the porch?" I asked, wanting to watch them. It was interesting to watch Cage with his teammates.

"I reckon, but when they come walking back this way, you go on inside. Ya hear?"

"Yes, sir," I replied. He still treated me as if I was a sixteen-year-old girl instead of a twenty-year-old woman. Part of it was my fault. I'd been so dependent on Josh that when he died, I'd crumbled. Daddy had to take care of me like I was a child again. I didn't remember to eat. I didn't answer phone calls. I didn't go anywhere. I gave him complete control over my life. My age didn't mean anything to him now. He still thought he had to take care of me. Until I moved out, I knew he would always feel that way.

A loud whistle broke into my thoughts, and I gazed back down toward the barn to see three of the guys sitting on the back of the farm truck staring up at me.

The blond one with long hair pulled back into a ponytail was prettier than the others, and he knew it. The flirtatious grin on his face and tilt of his head made it apparent that he really thought I'd just go walking down there because he whistled at me. Maybe all baseball players were full of themselves.

Cage came walking out of the barn, and his eyes locked on mine. He shifted his gaze to the guys on the truck and gave them a single shake of his head. All three of them said something to him, and he didn't look real happy. But they didn't look back up here at me. I wondered if he warned them off because I was Coach Mack's niece or because he didn't want them flirting with me.

Somehow I didn't think he'd really care if they flirted with me. He was a huge flirt. It was no surprise his friends were too.

The guys all started heading back this way now that Cage had on clean clothes. Daddy was back in his office, and I wondered if I could get away with sitting in the rocker while they passed by.

Cage led the group as they drew closer to the front of the house. I scanned the group, and then my eyes came back to him. He was watching me. I felt my face grow warm. What if he talked to me in front of all of them and I said something stupid and they all laughed at me? I decided I had better do what Daddy said after all. Turning, I grabbed the door handle and rushed inside.

I walked over to the fridge for a glass of water. I hated that something as stupid as a bunch of guys made me nervous. There was a knock on the screen door, and then it opened up a crack and Cage stuck his head in.

"Hey, you okay?" he asked with a concerned look on his face.

"Yeah, I'm fine," I replied, quickly feeling silly for running inside.

"I'm sorry about the guys. They didn't mean to make you uncomfortable. I was taking a shower, so I didn't know they were bothering you."

He had been worried about them making me uncomfortable? That was . . . sweet.

"Oh. No. It was fine. I don't even know what they said."

A crooked grin flashed on his face. "Probably a good thing. You sure are a pretty picture standing on the porch in them shorts. Can't say I blame them for staring."

My face felt flushed, and a horn blared outside.

"I gotta go. Just wanted to make sure you were okay," he said.

I nodded, and he stepped back and let the screen door close. Then he winked at me before turning and walking away.

Chapter Ten

EVA

I pulled the truck up to the lake and grabbed my towel and iPod. I intended to lie out for a couple of hours and even take a swim. I'd been doing everything I could think of to keep a distance from Cage. The past forty-eight hours had been exhausting

I straightened my towel out on the thickest patch of grass. I checked to make sure there were no snakes hiding out nearby. Growing up in the country, I'd learned a long time ago that snakes could be anywhere. Once I was sure I was nice and safe, I stuck my earbuds in and put my "After Josh" playlist on. I didn't actually title it "After Josh"—that was just how I thought of it. All the playlists I'd had before reminded me of him. So I'd found songs by artists we'd never listened to together and made myself a compilation of songs that didn't remind me of him at all. It was the only way I'd been able to start listening to music again.

I knew that Daddy and Jeremy both hoped I'd pick up my guitar again, but I knew that would never happen. The day I'd finally brought it back out of the closet and stood it in the corner where I'd used to keep it, Jeremy had been all smiles. Until he realized I wasn't actually going to play it. Every song I'd ever written had something to do with Josh. Even the ones that weren't love songs, Josh was in there somewhere. He was always my inspiration. I couldn't play it now. Not with him gone. It just never felt right.

At least I'd let music back into my life. That was a step I never thought I'd manage. Growing up with music as my second love—behind Josh, of course—I'd always thought it would be my future. Somehow I'd do something with my songs and ability. I knew now that I'd lost that love too. It was only a painful reminder now.

Rough fabric brushed my leg, and I sat straight up, ready to scream, when my eyes locked on a very amused Cage. Reaching up, I jerked my earbuds out and scowled at him. "You scared me!"

Cage tried to hold in his laughter, but his eyes were twinkling with it. "Yeah, sorry about that. I tried talking to you, but when you didn't respond, I figured you were either sleeping or that music was turned up real damn loud."

"What are you doing here?" I snapped. I was irritated. Mostly at myself, but he didn't know that.

"Well, I was driving back here to take a swim because it's hot, and I come upon you laid out here in a tiny hot-pink bikini. I'm a man, sugar, and I couldn't resist the view."

I stared down at myself, then back at him. He liked what he saw? I could not smile. I could not smile. I'd look like an idiot.

"Why don't you go for a swim with me? I'll even leave my boxers on."

Swim with Cage. Um. This was probably a bad idea.

"I don't know. . . ."

Cage stood up and began lifting his shirt off over his head, and all thought was lost. Was that a barbell in his nipple?

"What is that?" I asked, unable to take my eyes off the small silver bar that was definitely attached to his hard, tanned pec.

"It's a piercing, sweet Eva. Now get your sexy ass up and go swim with me. You gotta be hot."

I shook my head, still trying to figure out when he'd gotten a nipple piercing. "I've never seen it before," I finally stated.

Cage let out a small, sexy laugh. "Yeah, I know. I don't figure your daddy would be real keen on me having a nipple piercing. I keep it out for the most part while I'm here. But I put it in last night, and I just forgot to take it out this morning."

Here I always thought a guy getting his nipple pierced was gross. This was so not gross.

Cage began unlacing his work boots, and I watched as he slipped them off. When his hands went to his jeans, I knew I should stand up and act like this wasn't a striptease, but tearing my eyes away from Cage York stripping was just about impossible.

"You gonna get up and join me, or am I gonna have to pick you up and throw you in?"

When Cage's jeans slid down his hips and the dark blue of his boxers started to show, I jumped up and swung my gaze away from him to look out at the water.

Cage found this funny. His low chuckle made me feel flushed all over. I headed toward the water without looking back at his amused expression. Besides, I was pretty sure making eye contact with him would be difficult with that damn nipple piercing taunting me. One more reason to gawk at Cage's chest.

"You gonna tell me why you've been avoiding me the past couple of days?"

I dipped my toes into the water, testing the temperature. With the shade from the trees, our part of the lake remained cooler than other parts.

I tried to focus on the water and ignore his question. How was I supposed to answer that, anyway? I didn't want to tell him the truth: that I was embarrassed because I had smelled horrible, slept in his bed, and probably snored all night.

Shrugging, I stepped into the water and kept going until it

reached my waist. Then I turned back to look at Cage. He was standing on the bank with his eyes focused on me. The dark-blue boxers hung on his narrow hips, and the dark hair that began just below his navel had me swallowing hard.

"You wouldn't consider walking back out of the water and letting me stand here and watch, would ya?"

"What?" I asked, and he just smiled and shook his head.

"Never mind."

He held my gaze as he walked down into the cool water. I wanted to stare at his nipple again, but I wouldn't let myself. It would just give him one more thing to tease me about.

"Ah, sweet relief. My invisible fairy has left me high and dry the past two days. I've had to fend for myself for water, and all I've had to cool off with was the lake. Wonder what it was I did to piss her off?"

The laugh that bubbled up inside me surprised me. I hadn't laughed in so long, until Cage. He always knew how to make me laugh. How to make me forget.

"The invisible fairy was embarrassed by her behavior," I muttered, and sank deeper into the water.

"Why? What did she do?" he asked, following me out deeper into the water.

"She drank a little too much," I admitted.

Cage's eyes went wide in surprise. "Really? Fairies drink? I'll be damned. I had no idea. Would you mind letting her know

I don't hold it against her? I happen to have made some bad choices when tequila was involved."

His acceptance of my stupidity made something in me melt. Had I ever known anyone like him before? He made mistakes and fessed up to them. He didn't make excuses for the things he did wrong. He just dealt with it and went on. I wanted to be that strong. I wanted that kind of determination to just live.

"I wish I were more like you," I said before I could think about it.

Cage's eyes really did go wide with shock this time. "What?" he asked.

Shrugging, I dipped my head back to wet my hair and slick it back out of my face. "You heard me. You accept life and your mistakes, and you go on. I don't do that well."

"Don't say that, Eva. You don't want to be anything like me. I've done some fucked-up stuff. Made some really bad decisions. If I hadn't had Low there to keep me grounded, who knows? I'd probably be in jail by now."

Low? As in Willow the redhead? So she was his girlfriend? If Low had been the one to keep him from completely screwing up his life, then why the heck was he flirting with Becca Lynn and me? The old me would have stormed off in a huff. I didn't want to do that now. Josh would have run after me and tried to fix whatever was wrong. Cage wouldn't do that. He would expect me to tell him what was wrong. He wouldn't run after me. Cage York didn't run after women.

"Does Low know that you flirt with every attractive female you come in contact with?" I asked, trying hard not to sound jealous. Because I was not jealous. I was not.

"Hell yeah, she knows," he replied. The confused look in his pretty pale-blue eyes changed to understanding. "Oh, wait, you think Low and I have a thing?" He let out a loud, amused laugh. "Not even close. Low is engaged, and it ain't to me."

What was an engaged woman doing changing his sheets and bringing him towels? "She's awfully helpful when you need her. Does her fiancé know this?"

Cage smirked. "Yeah, he knows. When he got Low, he got her best friend too. Low and I grew up together. We both had shitty families in a shitty part of town. We watched out for each other. We were each other's family. She's the only family I got."

My heart ached a little at the picture he'd just painted with so few words. Two kids who only had each other. No parents or siblings to love them. I remembered Low's sweet smile and confused expression when I'd been so rude about the sheets. She probably thought I was a complete bitch.

"Oh," I replied. "I didn't realize that. I thought she was one of your many beck-and-call girls."

Cage roared with laughter. "Please don't ever let Low hear you say that. She'd go all redhead spitting mad." He took a step toward me, and his cocky smirk returned. "You think I got beck-and-call girls?" he asked.

I raised one eyebrow and returned his stupid smirk. "I know you have beck-and-call girls. Guys like you have them lined up and waiting."

Cage took another step toward me. "You think you have me all figured out, don't ya?"

I nodded and clenched my fist to keep from reaching out and touching his nipple barbell now that it was so close to me. So very tempting.

"There's a lot you don't know."

"Like what?" I asked, needing to get my mind off his nipple and abs so very close to my hands.

"Like the fact that I think you've got the prettiest damn eyes I've ever seen. I think about them way too often. Or that I told Low about you. I never tell Low about girls. They've never been important enough. And that Sunday night was the best fucking night of my life even if your drunk ass probably can't remember it."

"Oh" was the only response I had. My heart was beating so hard in my chest, I wondered if he could hear it.

"Speaking of engaged females . . ." Cage picked up my left hand, where my ring finger was now bare. I'd taken it off when I was drunk and tucked it away in my purse. Wearing Josh's ring while I drank tequila shots and danced in a bar just felt wrong. I hadn't put it back on.

"There's a lot you don't know about me, too," I murmured.

Most guys would press for more. But not Cage. He just accepted what I wanted to tell him and didn't ask for what I wasn't ready to give.

Cage's chest was so close to me now, it brushed up against my breast. I gave in. I couldn't help it. He'd just said I had the prettiest eyes he'd ever seen and that sleeping with me was the best night of his life. Reaching up, I brushed my thumb over the small silver bar. Cage's pec muscle jumped. I took that as encouragement. I ran my fingertip around it slowly. His chest began rising faster with each quick intake of breath. Knowing that I was affecting Cage gave me an odd sense of power. His touch always sent me into a tizzy. It was nice to reverse the roles.

"You really like that nipple piercing, don't you?" he said in something close to a growl.

"Mm-hmm, I've never seen one before. I like it a lot."

"I'm not complaining. If it fascinates you that much, I'll go get the other one done too." His breathing was jagged.

The naughty girl inside me, who I honestly didn't know existed, bent my head down and looked up at him through my lashes as I flicked it with my tongue.

"Ah, shit," he whispered, but it almost sounded like a moan.

Encouraged by his response, I flattened my tongue and ran it up and over his hard nipple.

CAGE

Nothing. Absolutely nothing I'd ever experienced was as hot as Eva licking my nipple like it was a damn lollipop. She had my dick so hard, there was no way I was going to be able to get rid of this thing without some relief. Cold water wasn't going to be enough this time. I was going to need some serious private time real fucking soon.

"Can I watch you get the other one?" she asked, staring up at me with those eyes of hers through heavily lidded lashes. Damn. What had she just said? I couldn't keep my train of thought straight.

"Huh?" I managed to ask.

She began placing small kisses around my pec. "Can I go with you when you get the other one done?" she asked with her lips against my chest.

"Baby, I'll let you sit in my damn lap if you want to," I replied.

She giggled, and her sexy little tongue went right back to flicking the barbell. I deserved a damn award for not having her perky titties out of that bikini top and giving her nipples the same attention she was giving mine.

"I'd like that," she whispered.

"I'm real glad you like it, but I don't think I can take much more."

She stopped and raised her eyes to meet mine. "Does it hurt?"

Fuck, she was innocent. "No, sweetheart, it feels amazing. But I want your pretty little nipples in my mouth real damn bad right about now."

She froze. I waited for her to back away and run for the shore, back to safety.

If she left me here, I was jacking off right here in this damn water. I wouldn't be able to get far with the insane throbbing between my legs.

"Okay," she said so softly I wondered if I'd heard her right. She reached back and undid the strings holding her top up as I watched. I was afraid I was going to wake up any minute alone in my bed and horny as hell.

She pulled the small piece of fabric covering her tits away and laid it over my shoulder. They were perfect: round and soft, just a little more than a handful. I covered each one and held their weight in my hands. This might never happen again, and if this was all I was going to get of Eva Brooks, then I was going to savor every damn minute.

Eva gasped as my hands squeezed gently, then softly pinched the round cherry nipples on each tip. "I'm gonna put them in my mouth now, Eva," I warned as I lowered my head to the right breast and pulled her nipple into my mouth. Fuck, it was like candy. Her fingers ran through my hair and grasped handfuls, holding on to my head firmly as I sucked and kneaded each breast.

"Ahhh," she moaned, pressing closer. The handfuls of my hair she held tightly in her fist were being pulled just enough to make it feel good. I trailed kisses across her breastbone and licked hungrily at the dip between her breasts. I could do this all damn day and not get enough.

Eva's leg lifted up to wrap around my waist, and she pressed up against my incredibly eager cock. Ah, hell no, she couldn't do that.

"Eva, what're you doing, sweetheart?" I asked as I closed my eyes tightly, trying hard to press my needy dick harder against the warm V of her legs.

"I wanna feel more," she moaned as she lifted her other leg and locked her legs behind my back. Her heat pressed firmly against me now, and my knees buckled at the intensity.

"Ohfuck," I muttered as Eva began rocking her hips gently. The moment she found the right fit, she cried out and rocked harder.

Motherfuckinghell. Her tits began bouncing as she rode me. I'd heard of dry humping, but I'd never experienced it. Hell, it felt good. With each slide of her crotch up and down against my dick, I trembled. Her head was thrown back, and she was completely lost. I wanted those sweet tits in my mouth again, but watching her was amazing. Her swollen mouth was slightly open, and the expression on her face was one of pure ecstasy.

"Ohgodohgodohgod," she began to chant as she lifted her head and heavy lidded eyes met mine. I needed that mouth. Leaning forward, I covered her lips with mine, thrusting my tongue between their plump softness and began making love to her mouth the way I wanted to make love to her body.

As she rocked against my dick, I slipped my hands under her bottom and pulled her in tighter against me. The moment I felt her tense under my hands, I knew she was close. Pulling back just enough to see her eyes as she shattered, I pressed one more kiss to her mouth.

And she came apart in my hands.

EVA

I slid down Cage's body, but he kept his hands firmly on my waist. He thought I was going to try to escape. Part of me wanted to go run and hide, but the biggest part wanted to stay right here and enjoy the tremors still running through my body.

Cage bent his head and rested his forehead against mine. We didn't say anything. It wasn't an awkward silence; it was nice. No words were really needed.

He reached for the bikini top he had tied around his arm at some point and began putting it back on me.

"I need to cover you back up," he whispered. I started to help him, but he pushed my hands away. "No. I want to do this."

Reminding myself that Cage was just good with females because he had been with a lot of them was hard. I wanted to believe he was just this sweet and romantic with me. For now I could pretend.

Once he had it tied behind my back, he adjusted the cups over my breasts and brushed his thumbs over the tops of them before dropping his hands to his side.

"I gotta get back to work before your daddy comes looking for me." I could hear the regret in Cage's voice, and it made me smile. He didn't want to leave me.

"Okay, that's probably a good idea," I agreed, and started toward the shore.

When Cage didn't move, I turned back around to see him standing there watching me. "You coming?"

A wicked grin touched his lips. "Not yet."

Shaking my head in confusion, I smiled and headed back toward the shore. I no longer needed to hide out, so I picked up my towel and headed for my truck. When I climbed inside, I saw Cage still standing out in the water watching me. What was he doing? A sexy smirk touched his lips, and he saluted me as I backed up and drove away.

I pulled the frozen towel out of the freezer and picked up the fresh thermos of lemonade I'd prepared for Cage. He had returned an hour ago, and I'd waited until he was busy to take his things out to him. It wasn't that I wanted to avoid him as much as it was that I liked the game it had turned into. He wanted to catch me leaving him the towel and fresh drink. I preferred to remain the invisible fairy. Smiling, I headed for the door. Just then it swung open and Daddy walked inside.

"You bringing that to me?" he asked, staring down at the ice towel like the ones he kept in the freezer for himself. I never took things out to Daddy. He always came inside when he was hot and thirsty. Cage didn't do that. He just stayed outside in the heat.

"Um . . ." I wasn't sure how to answer this. I didn't want to lie to him, because I was pretty sure he'd see right through me and make a bigger deal out of this than it was.

Daddy stood there frowning at me, and I knew I needed to answer him before he came up with the worst possible scenario.

"Cage won't come inside when he gets thirsty or hot. I haven't been real welcoming. So when he is busy, I go leave him a towel and a drink so I don't have to talk to him."

That was the truth, or at least, it was up until about an hour ago in the lake.

Daddy let out a sigh and nodded. "You're a good girl, Eva. That boy probably ain't had a whole lot of, if any, extra care taken with him. He's a hard worker, though, that's for sure. Guess I should've been worrying about him overheating and dehydrating." He stepped around me and patted me on the back.

He wasn't going to get mad about this. Relaxing, I let out a quiet sigh of relief and took a step toward the door.

"Don't mean he's good enough for you. Keeping your distance is what you need to do. Just 'cause he's a good worker don't mean he ain't dangerous to a pretty young girl. Especially an innocent."

I couldn't agree with him. I knew better. Cage wasn't dangerous at all. He was nothing like Daddy assumed. Nodding was the best I could do. I stepped outside into the heat and headed down to the barn.

Cage rounded the truck shirtless and carrying a shovel. I almost tripped over myself. His nipple was bare again. As much as I liked looking at the piercing, I was thankful. He was right about Daddy. He wouldn't like it much. Cage stopped walking when he saw me coming, and a grin instantly lit up his face. Reminding myself that Daddy was probably watching from the window of the kitchen, I knew we would have to play this cool.

"What's this? Eva Brooks bringing me an ice towel and a thermos of water? Better watch it, my invisible fairy will get jealous. She's the possessive sort."

I had to bite my lip hard to keep from smiling. "She'll get over it. And it isn't water, it's lemonade," I said, setting it down on the tailgate of the truck.

His eyes left me and scanned the yard. He was looking for Daddy.

"He's watching us from the kitchen window. Just take it. I'll see you later." I gave him a small smile, then turned and headed right back to the house. I just hoped he wasn't watching me walk away. Daddy wouldn't like that at all.

"Thanks!" he called from behind me, and I kept on walking.

Chapter Eleven

CAGE

For three days she'd been gone. Three very long days. When I'd woken up to find a letter had been left beside my bed, I'd been hoping it was a sexy letter letting me know when I would get to be alone with her again. Instead it was a letter telling me that Jeremy was coming to get her and take her to visit his family in Louisiana and that she'd be back in a couple of days.

I had been anxious since she'd left. I knew he was telling her about his plans, and it was making me nervous as shit. I didn't like thinking about her being off somewhere and upset. Reminding myself that Jeremy knew how to deal with her emotions just fine was hard.

Low would be here to get me in the morning, and I didn't want to leave without seeing Eva first. I wouldn't enjoy my day off without knowing she was okay. How did I not have her damn phone number? I'd slept all night with her in my arms and I'd given her an orgasm in the lake. I didn't normally plan on seeing girls again, or if I did, I never asked for their numbers unless they knew the score. Eva didn't fall into either of those categories. She was . . . more. I needed her fucking cell number.

I stepped out of the shower and wrapped a towel around my waist. Maybe I could call Low and see if she just wanted to do something around here for a few hours. I didn't have to go check on my apartment. The idea of hanging out with Preston and picking up girls on the beach no longer held the same appeal. Eva Brooks was screwing with my head.

I picked up my phone and pressed Low's speed dial number.

"Cage?"

"Yeah, you good?"

Larissa squealed in the background and started clapping while calling my name.

"Someone wants to talk to you. Hold on."

Smiling, I waited for Larissa's little voice. I hadn't seen her since I'd come out here. Larissa was Low's niece. Until Larissa's father had decided to become part of her life, I'd helped Low take care of Larissa while Larissa's mother did other things. At times it was like Larissa was Low's child. Things changed, though, once Low's fiancé, Marcus, walked into her life. Now

Larissa came to visit Low only when Low asked for her. She wasn't forced to be her niece's parent anymore.

"Hey, Cage," Larissa said into the phone.

"Hey, baby girl. You having fun with Low?"

"Yes! Martus here too!" she yelled into the phone. She hadn't figured out yet that she could just speak normally into the phone.

"Then I bet you're getting all kinds of attention. How are all your princesses doing?"

"Got a new one! Martus buyed me Media. Her has Low Low's hair."

I had no idea what that meant, but I wasn't about to tell her that. "You'll have to show me next time I see you."

Low started talking, and Larissa told me, "Bye."

"Did you get that thing about the new princess's hair?" Low asked with an amused voice.

"Nope."

"Didn't think you would. Disney has a new princess. Her name is Merida, and her hair is long, red, and curly. It is much messier than mine, but Marcus is having entirely too much fun with it. He's bought Larissa several Merida things and calls her Princess Low instead."

The happiness in her voice made everything that was wrong feel right. She'd been handed one shithole life. Now things had changed, and Low had finally gotten a break.

"I can't wait to see this new redheaded princess."

"Hmmm, but that isn't why you called. What's up?"

"I need . . ." I turned around to see Eva standing in the door-way with an odd expression on her face. "Uh, let me call you back." I ended the call and walked over to take Eva's hand and pull her inside so I could close the door behind her. "Hey, you're back."

She stared up at me with a softness I wasn't expecting. "Did I just hear you talk to a little girl about her princesses?"

How long had she been standing there?

"Yeah, it was Low's niece, Larissa."

"And you talk to her on the phone about her dolls? I really don't know you at all, Cage York."

I reached out and wrapped one of her long curls around my finger. I just needed to touch her somehow. "You're back," I repeated.

She tried to smile and failed. I could see the small wobble in her bottom lip.

"What's wrong?" I asked, already knowing this was about Jeremy.

A small tear escaped, and I quickly swiped it away with my finger.

"Jeremy is moving," she said. "He needs to. I want him to. I mean, he needs to live his life." She swallowed hard, then closed her eyes tightly. "I knew he was moving before he told me. Seeing his apartment and his new life just was a lot to take in. I'm happy for him, but I'm going to miss him. I'll be lost without him."

I pulled her into my arms, and she buried her face in my shoulder. The warm tears splashed against my skin, and each drop broke my heart. I'd fix this if I knew how. I just didn't know what to do that could make this any better. Jeremy was her safety net.

"It's just that," she choked out, "he's moving on. He's forgetting." She stopped herself and pulled back from me. I could see the pain in her eyes and the desire to tell me about Josh. I wanted her to. I wanted to be able to talk to her about it. I hated that she felt like she only had Jeremy to run to.

"What's he forgetting, Eva?" I asked. She'd avoided telling me anything more about the fact that she'd taken off her engagement ring. I was trying so hard to keep her from running from me, but I needed more now.

"The past," she finally replied. Turning around, she reached for the doorknob. Fuck. She was gonna run.

"Don't," I begged. "Stay. Talk to me."

She didn't turn back around. Instead she opened the door and walked away.

EVA

Cage hadn't returned until after midnight Sunday night. The only reason I knew this was because the last time I'd looked at the clock by my bed, it had said it was 12:05 a.m. Shortly after,

I'd fallen asleep. By the time I'd gotten up Monday morning, Cage was already out with the cows. Daddy was having him tag the ones he was sending to the stockyard. I'd gone down to the lake, hoping he'd come looking for me, but after three hours I realized I'd pushed him too far.

He'd been open with me from the beginning. He hadn't held back anytime I asked him something. I knew so much more about him than he knew about me. That was my fault. How did I tell him about Josh? How did I explain to another guy that losing Josh broke me? How would I deal with seeing the pity in Cage's eyes when he looked at me? I just didn't think I could handle it. Jeremy was moving on, but I couldn't.

I'd gone back to delivering Cage's towel and thermos anonymously. He obviously didn't want to see me. I'd walked out on him when he'd asked me not to go. The pleading sound in his voice haunted my dreams.

He wasn't the hard, selfish playboy I'd expected when I'd first met him. Cage was gentle when he needed to be. The way his voice had gone all sweet when he'd talked to the little girl on the phone and the way he'd so willingly pulled me into his arms without question to comfort me when he realized I was upset proved it.

When he'd noticed my ring was missing, he'd asked me about it, and I'd ignored it and distracted him. He hadn't pushed for more then either. Cage had put up with a lot from me. He'd had enough.

I pulled my legs up so I could wrap my arms around them and rest my chin on my knees. I had grown so pathetic over the past few days just trying to get a glimpse of Cage that I spent more time on the rocker on the porch than I did anywhere else.

Gravel crunched, and I watched as Becca Lynn's little red convertible swung into the driveway. She'd stayed away longer than I'd expected. We had talked about Cage very little before we'd started drinking shots of tequila the night we went out.

Today her boots were candy-apple red. Almost a perfect match to her car. She'd probably been aware of that when she bought them. Knowing Becca, she'd asked to take a boot outside and compare colors so she got it just right.

"Well, look at you, sitting out here in the rocking chair like you're sixty years old," Becca teased as she pranced across the front yard and up the steps.

"It's a nice spot," I replied. One where I could catch glimpses of Cage.

Becca Lynn pursed her red lips together, also a pretty dang close match to her boots, and scanned the yard. "Don't see your badass help anywhere," she chirped.

"His name is Cage. You know that," I snapped.

Becca swung her gaze back to me. "Oooooh, testy. Did you go and get a soft spot for the resident hottie?"

"He's not such a bad guy after all. He didn't take advantage of you, did he?"

Becca stiffened, then shrugged as if she couldn't care less. "I think he's probably one of those smoking-hot but very gay types. Normally, when a guy is that pretty, he is too good to be true. My guess is, he has an equally beautiful partner back home. Don't get me wrong, I'm so not a homophobe. I think it would be hot as shit to see. But it's a shame such perfection bats for the other team."

She did not just accuse Cage of being gay because he wouldn't screw her after just meeting her. I wanted to scream just how not gay Cage was, but I controlled myself.

"I've seen the girl in his life. He isn't gay," I informed her. She didn't have to know Willow was engaged to someone else.

Becca frowned. "He has a girlfriend?" she asked, pulling herself up to sit on the porch railing.

Technically, yes. He had a girl who was a friend. "They've grown up together. Been together for years."

Becca's face went sad, and it dawned on me what I'd just said. She was thinking about me and Josh. This was the pity I didn't ever want to see on Cage's face. I got enough pity from everyone else. Jeremy was the only one who hadn't pitied me. He'd stood by me and mourned with me, but he'd never pitied me.

"Jeremy's going to LSU in the fall," I blurted out, needing to tell someone and needing to change the subject. I wasn't in the mood to discuss Josh with her.

"Oh, wow." Becca was watching me closely. She was waiting

on me to break down and cry. I'd done that already. For two full days I'd cried every time I thought about him moving on. I was done with the tears. They weren't tears of sadness over losing Jeremy. They were tears of sadness because he had found a way to move on and I was still stuck, unable to move past Josh. "So, when did you find out?" she asked.

"Last week. He took me to see his new place. He's leasing an apartment with his cousin from Jefferson Parish. He leaves for good next month. He needs to find a job and get settled in before school starts."

"You two gonna be okay apart?"

What she really meant was would I be okay without him. Everyone seemed to understand that Jeremy was ready to get on with his life.

"We'll be fine. Jeremy needs to live."

Becca nodded. "Yeah, he does." She paused. "And so do you."

I wish I knew how.

The rumble of a truck interrupted us, and Becca turned from her perch on the railing to watch as Cage's truck pulled up from the pasture.

"God, I hope he has his shirt off," she whispered.

I was in agreement with that wish.

When he stepped out of the truck, he looked our way but quickly shifted his gaze, then walked into the barn. He was wearing a white T-shirt that looked a little too small. I wondered if he was wearing it because he had his barbell in.

"I'm going to go talk to him. I'll be back," Becca announced as she jumped down from the railing and started down the stairs.

What if he was changing? What if she saw his pierced nipple? I didn't want her to see it. It was my secret. I opened my mouth to say something to stop her, but I didn't have an excuse other than that I didn't want to share him. How ridiculous was that? I watched helplessly as Becca Lynn headed toward the barn door. Short of running after her and tackling her to the ground, I couldn't do anything about this.

Chapter Twelve

CAGE

I'd made it three days without breaking down and going after her. I wasn't sure how much longer I could wait her out. She'd run, and I wanted her to be the one to come back. But dammit, seeing her sitting there on that porch with her eyes on me so big and sad was more than any man could withstand.

I slammed my bedroom door closed and stalked over to ram my fist into the wall. I needed to get my frustration out somehow. I cared too much. Way too damn much. This was different from caring for Low. Completely different. Eva had me wrapped up in knots. I didn't do commitment. I wasn't a one-woman guy. I liked variety. I liked not having to give a shit. This caring stuff was bullshit. I didn't need this.

A knock on the door startled me, and hope soared in my

chest. She'd finally come back. Two long strides and I was at the door, jerking it open, ready to fall on my knees and promise to do whatever the hell she wanted me to do in order to make her happy.

"Hey, Cage," Becca Lynn said cheerily as my excitement turned to bitterness.

"Becca," I replied.

"Um, can I come in?" she asked. I looked behind her to make sure Eva wasn't standing there waiting to talk to me. Where had Becca come from, anyway? Had she been on the porch with Eva?

"I guess." I stepped back. Hopefully the lack of enthusiasm in my tone would keep her from doing anything stupid.

"Um, so, how have you been?" she asked as she stepped inside and closed the door behind her.

"Good."

She walked over and sat down on the edge of my bed. The way she was sticking her tits out in my direction, she was offering herself up for whatever I might want to do. A couple of weeks ago, before I'd arrived here and been completely thrown off balance by Eva, I would've been all over that. Not now. Things had changed for me.

"I'm sorry I haven't been around since the night at the lake. I guess I don't take rejection well," she cooed.

"Guess not," I grunted, and kept my distance from her.

Becca Lynn reached down to take the hem of her tank top and started pulling it up.

"Don't, Becca. I'm not interested. I told you before that you're a nice girl and real pretty, but just not my type."

Becca ripped her shirt off anyway and threw it back on her bed. Her bare tits were nice, but after having seen Eva's, they paled in comparison.

"I know about your girlfriend. I'm not going to tell anyone," she purred as she reached down and began playing with her nipples.

"What girlfriend?" I asked, confused.

Becca Lynn smiled brightly up at me. "The one you've grown up with all your life. Eva told me about her."

Eva had told Becca I had a girlfriend? She'd used Low as the "girlfriend" so she wouldn't actually be lying. I couldn't keep the grin off my face. She hadn't wanted Becca to come in here. She'd been jealous.

I wasn't waiting on her to give in and come to me. This wasn't about games anymore. I wanted to talk to Eva—now. I needed her to tell me everything. Even if I already knew it, I wanted her to tell me. It was time she stopped running and faced her fears.

"Where are you going?" Becca Lynn asked, and I glanced back at her now, standing in my room topless and confused.

"Put your shirt on, Becca Lynn, and run on along."

I didn't wait for her to throw something at me or call me names. I'd heard all that before. I just wanted to find Eva.

Opening the barn door, I looked back up at the porch and found her still sitting there. Our gazes locked, and I motioned toward the lake with a tilt of my head. I waited until she nodded in agreement, and then I headed for the truck. It was time we got this shit straightened out.

EVA

As soon as Cage pulled away in the truck, Becca Lynn came stomping out of the barn with a snarl on her face. Relief washed over me. When she'd gone in there, I'd let one bad scenario after another play in my head until Cage had come out of the barn door like he was on a mission. Knowing he wanted me to meet him down at the lake made the butterflies in my stomach act up.

"He's a complete ass. I don't know why I even bother." Becca Lynn stalked past the porch toward her car.

"You leaving?" I asked, just to be sure before I followed Cage.

"Yeah, I got crap to do. I'll call you," Becca replied.

Once she spun out of the driveway, I jumped up and ran for the truck, but I stopped before I reached the door. Turning around, I stared at the garage. My Jeep sat in there unused. I'd taken off my ring. It was time I drove my Jeep. Slowly, I made my way toward the garage. I wasn't sure if the memories would prove too much for me. I pressed the code on the door, and it raised and rolled back. My silver Jeep was nice and clean. I knew my dad paid Jeremy to take it out once every other week to wash it and make sure it cranked. I pretended like I didn't know this, because confronting them about it would just make me remember.

The need to crumple to the ground and weep was gone. I had only fond memories to hold close. I walked around and opened the driver's-side door. "Guess it's time to drive you again," I whispered as I climbed behind the wheel and cranked it up. Country music blared from the radio, and I smiled thinking about Jeremy blaring the music so he could hear it while he cleaned it.

I backed out of the drive and headed down to the lake without any problem. No moments of intense pain and loss. Just me and my Jeep.

I saw Cage's truck as soon as I turned the corner around the old maple trees. He was sitting on the tailgate waiting for me. His eyes widened in surprise as I pulled up beside him. He'd never seen my Jeep. All he'd seen me drive was one of Dad's old farm trucks. I smiled at his expression, then hopped down and walked over to him.

"Nice wheels," he said when I stopped in front of him.

"Thanks," I replied, before pulling myself up to sit on the tailgate with him.

"In case you're curious, Becca Lynn stripped off her top after I asked her not to. I never went near her, and I walked out on her. She's probably pissed."

I couldn't hold back my laugh. "Yeah, she is."

"You think that's funny?" Cage asked, trying to sound stern, but the teasing tone in his voice was unmistakable.

"Yes. I do."

Cage grinned, then looked down at the ground. I knew he was waiting on me. He may have asked me to come out here, but it was because he was still waiting on answers. He deserved them.

"I was engaged . . . ," I started, but couldn't find the right words.

Cage didn't pressure me but waited silently beside me.

"Josh died in Baghdad a year and a half ago," I managed to say without choking up.

Cage didn't turn his head to look at me. There was no pity, and there were no empty condolences. I wasn't sure what I'd expected from him, but his calm acceptance of this wasn't it.

"I know. Jeremy told me the Friday before your drunken escapade."

Jeremy had told him? Why?

"But you never said anything," I said, trying to wrap my head around the fact that Jeremy had betrayed me. He'd broken a confidence. He had known I didn't want Cage to know.

"I wanted you to tell me." He finally shifted his gaze off the ground and turned his head to look at me. There was no pity in his pale blue depths, just understanding. "It was your story. If you wanted me to know, you'd tell me. Then when you didn't after that day in the lake, I was angry. Hurt. I'd hoped you understood that this wasn't a game to me."

He'd known for a while. Never once had he treated me differently. He hadn't handled me with kid gloves. I reached over and covered his hand with mine. He flipped his over and threaded his fingers through mine, then squeezed.

"When you came to my room upset the other night, I knew why. I wanted to be the one to hold you while you cried and dealt with the coming change. But you wouldn't let me in. I've never wanted in, Eva. Not until you."

Swallowing was hard with the lump forming in my throat. I needed to tell him more. If we were going to have a summer fling, just be friends, or whatever we were going to end up being for the next two months, I wanted him to know.

"He was my best friend. We'd been inseparable since we were five years old. He was my first kiss. My first date." I felt the familiar burn in my nose as my eyes filled with tears. I had to do this. I had to share this with him. "We were going to grow old together. But he didn't come home." Cage released his hold on my hand and slipped his arm around my shoulder, pulling me up against his side. I laid my head on his chest and let the last tears I knew I would cry over Josh Beasley fall.

We didn't talk. He didn't ask me for more than I was willing to share. Instead he just held me. His hand gently rubbed up and down my arm, and he placed kisses on my head from time to time. Other than that, we just sat there in silence.

After I'd left Cage at the lake, I came back up to the house and went to my room. The guitar sat in the corner in its case, reminding me daily that it was once a part of me too. I'd managed to take off the ring. I'd conquered driving the Jeep. I wanted to play again. I closed my bedroom door and walked over to my bed, directly across from the guitar case. The stickers that Josh had bought me over the years covered every square inch of the black case. I'd hated the black case when Daddy had brought it home. When I'd outgrown my first guitar, he'd gone to buy me a new one. I'd wanted a cool case. The simple black case had been so boring. Josh had come over that night to see my new guitar and I'd told him how unhappy I was with the ugly case. The next day he'd shown up with a couple of funny bumper stickers and put them on the case. I'd laughed and told him it was perfect. Over the next couple of years he'd brought me stickers from places he went, or just random ones he'd come across and thought I'd like.

This was going to be the hardest hurdle, but I'd lost so much when Josh had died. I wanted to get some of it back. My music was something I missed. Reaching for the case, I picked it up and laid it down on the bed beside me. My heart picked up its pace as I opened the lid slowly and took in the sight of the smooth wood and familiar pick stuck in the strings. The notebook where all my songs were written was tucked safely under the neck. I wouldn't play those songs. Not yet. Small steps.

With reverence I took my old friend out of its velvet-lined case. Tonight I would just tune it. That would be enough for now. Holding it in my arms, I closed my eyes at the familiar feeling. It was as if I'd come home. My eyes stung with unshed tears as the emotion that came with being able to hold it in my arms again sank in.

I began tuning it as I strummed each string. The simple melody surrounded me. The world around me fell away. Just like before, it was just me and my music. Every emotion I'd held inside over the past year and a half began to bleed out into the music. I played through my sorrow, my anger, my bitterness, my forgiveness, and finally the hope that was slowly taking root inside me.

My out-of-practice fingers began to numb, and I slowed to a stop. The wetness on my face surprised me. They weren't sad tears. Not this time. This time they were happy tears. Maybe there would be a tomorrow after all.

The sound of clapping startled me, and I opened my eyes to see my daddy standing in the doorway. His eyes were watery, and a smile tilted up each corner of his mouth. "That's my girl," he said in a husky voice thick with emotion. "You don't know how good it was to come inside and hear that sound." He pressed his lips together tightly and inhaled deeply through his nose. "I look forward to hearing more of that." He nodded once in approval and then headed on down the hall to his room.

Chapter Thirteen

CAGE

I pulled Eva's badass little Jeep into the parking spot reserved for my apartment unit. Eva's dad was gone for the weekend on a deep-sea fishing trip, so I'd brought her home with me. The moment I'd finished work, I'd washed up and changed and we'd headed out. I wanted her to go out with me tonight and meet my friends. I also wanted her in my bed. My nice big king-size bed. Having her in my space suddenly seemed real damn important.

"It's right on the water?" Eva gasped as I reached behind her seat and grabbed her small suitcase.

"Yep, and I intend to get you out on that beach in your hot little bikini with me while we're here."

She smirked at me, then opened her door and got out.

I walked around the back of the Jeep so I could grab her hand. The idea of her being here made me ridiculously happy.

"It's almost nine. Will your friends still be out? Or will everything be closed?" she asked as I led her to the stairs. Innocent little country girl was used to everything closing down with the sunset.

"We're at the beach, Eva. There's a nightlife here. I doubt anyone is even at Live Bay yet. Band doesn't normally get started until ten."

"Oh" was her simple reply.

When we reached the door to my apartment, I unlocked it and prayed Low had gotten someone over here to clean it for me. I knew Preston had used it a few times last week, and I didn't know what he might have left behind. The fresh smell of Pine-Sol hit my nose and I relaxed.

"It's so big." Eva breathed in awe. I looked around and didn't think it was all that big, but I wasn't going to argue with her.

"Oh, and you can see the water," she squealed, and ran over to the window overlooking the gulf.

I set her bag down on the new leather couch I'd hardly used since I'd bought it. I needed a kiss. Eva was here all in my personal space and I wanted to celebrate.

"Come here," I whispered as I came up behind her and turned her around to face me.

I dipped my head down so I could press a few soft kisses

to her lips, then reached up and cupped her face with both my hands before I deepened the kiss. Her eager mouth opened willingly, and the taste of her made me just a little crazy. It always did. Being this close to her just got better each time. Her two hands crept up my shirt until she found the barbell I'd inserted back into my nipple just for her after my shower. I'd wondered how long it would take her to search it out.

I grinned against her lips, and a small laugh escaped her. She thought my nipple ring was naughty, and something about that fascinated her.

Eva pulled back and looked up at me. "What time do we need to leave?" she asked, still rubbing her thumb over my nipple. It was a little hard to form coherent words when she did that.

"In about thirty minutes," I replied.

With a sigh, she stepped back out of my embrace. "Then I need you to direct me to a bathroom so I can freshen up and change."

"You can change in my bedroom. I'll even help you. It's full-service around here," I replied, reaching out to take her hand and pull her back toward me.

Shaking her head, she backed up just out of my grasp. "If you want to take me to meet your friends, then I need to get ready."

"You look incredible just like that, but if you must go change, then use the bathroom off the kitchen."

I watched her as she grabbed her bag and headed back to my room. I had never actually brought a girl here like this before. Low didn't count, and every other female who had been in my apartment had been with someone. They weren't here to get dressed in my room or sleep in my bed. Not once had I ever considered it. Bringing girls into my personal space had never appealed to me.

EVA

The parking lot was packed with cars. I tugged on the hem of my black skirt. I wasn't sure how everyone would be dressed. Cage wasn't much help in choosing an outfit. He liked everything I tried on, and he was wearing a pair of jeans and a snug-fitting light-blue T-shirt that did amazing things for his eyes.

He had driven my Jeep here because he'd said he'd need to park it. Now I understood why. He pulled around back into the "Employees Only" parking.

"What are you doing?" I asked, horrified. I was not leaving my Jeep here to get towed.

Cage reached over and squeezed my knee. "Relax, baby. I'll make sure they know this is my car. It'll be just fine."

I wasn't so sure about that. He opened the door and got out. I wasn't okay with this. Cage walked around the front of the Jeep and opened my door. "Get your pretty little behind out of this Jeep." He stepped up and slid his hands over the tops of my legs. "Or we could stay out here a little while longer and I could enjoy this skirt you decided to wear."

Laughing, I slapped at his hands. "I want to go in, but I'm worried about my Jeep."

Loud squealing startled me, and I snapped my head up to see a skinny blonde with very little clothing on and really large boobs running toward us. I was a little afraid her boobs were going to bounce right out of her top. What was she doing?

"Caaaaage!" she added to her loud squeal. Unsure who she was, I waited. Cage turned around at the sound of his name.

"Pris," he replied as she barreled into his arms. "Whoa, girl." He grabbed her by the waist. I wasn't sure if he was doing it because he wanted to or because he was trying to keep her from knocking them both down. She didn't seem real steady on the hot-pink six-inch platform stilettos she was wearing.

"Where have you been?" she asked, running her hands down his chest like she was ready to get him naked right now out here in the parking lot.

"I'm working out of town for the summer." He reached up and pulled her hands off his body.

She pouted when he put her hands back down at her side and took a step back from her. Was she for real? Her bottom lip was stuck out so far she might step on it with those ridiculous heels.

"But you're back tonight?"

"Yeah, just for tonight," he replied, shifting his body again until his back was touching my legs.

The blonde's eyes finally tore themselves away from Cage, and she focused on me. "Oh, you already got someone for the night." She started to pout, but then a slow smile appeared and she leaned into Cage and made sure she rubbed her breasts up his chest. "You know I don't mind sharing. We could do a three-some. I know how you like one girl to—"

"Uh, *no*. Bad idea," Cage interrupted her, and reached back to pick me up by my waist, then set me down beside him. He kept his arm wrapped protectively around me like he might need to keep me out of harm's way.

"Why not? Is she not—"

"Because that isn't my scene anymore. You can do something for me, though. Make sure parking knows the Jeep is mine."

The girl frowned, slightly confused, then nodded. "Okay. I will. But call me!"

Cage had already started walking us toward a back door.

"Who was that? And did you really have a threesome? Like with two girls at once?" I couldn't believe what I'd heard. I mean, I knew people talked about them, but I didn't think they actually did them. Eww.

"That was Priscilla. She's a waitress here. Let's not discuss my past sex life. I made a lot of mistakes; let's leave it at that."

My jaw dropped. "You so did have a threesome. Ohmygod." I breathed as he sighed at my reaction and opened the door for me to go inside.

The Cage I knew and the Cage that girl knew didn't even seem like the same guy. "Come this way," he said as he placed his hand on the small of my back and led me down a hall toward loud music. "Jackdown is playing tonight. I have friends in the band. They aren't the best, but they don't suck."

"You have friends in a band. No wonder you've had threesomes." I couldn't let that one go. How many girls had he actually been with?

"There they are," he said with obvious excitement in his voice. He called out over the noise, "Bring me two." He dropped his eyes to look at me. "Wait. What do you want to drink?"

"Coke," I replied. He studied me a moment, then nodded and looked back up at the bartender, who was standing a good distance off but watching Cage for his order. "Make that one and a Coke," he called out again.

Somehow the man heard him over the noise. We walked around the moving bodies instead of through them. I wasn't sure what to expect of Cage's friends after meeting the girl outside. Would they all be wild like that? Had I made a mistake coming here?

"Cage has arrived," a surfer-dude-looking blond guy announced with a huge grin on his face. "And he already found himself a babe, and dayum did he do good." The blond winked at me.

"Eva, the idiot who needs a haircut is Preston. He's also the same idiot who whistled at you the day the team came over," Cage informed me, leaning down so he didn't have to yell.

"Eva," Preston repeated. "I remember you now. I couldn't get a good look at you from a distance that day, but my instincts were right."

"He was dropped on his head as a baby. Ignore him," Cage whispered, making me laugh.

"Hey, Eva, I'm Trisha." A curvy platinum blonde with a pair of the plumpest lips I'd ever seen introduced herself. She seemed nice enough.

"Hello, it's nice to meet you," I replied. It was official: Every female Cage knew was blond and had a set of double Ds.

"This is my husband, Rock," she informed me, and I shifted my gaze to meet the amused eyes of a large, muscular, tattooed bald guy. He wasn't bad-looking if you liked the biker look.

"Low and Marcus coming?" Cage asked as he scanned the packed house.

"Not tonight," Trisha replied. "Marcus is taking some summer courses online, so Low is staying home with him."

"You wanna dance?" Cage's mouth was so close to my ear, the warmth from his breath made me shiver. I looked back out at the dance floor, and all those people moving in ways I'd never really seen intimidated me.

"Not really," I said, shifting my gaze back to his. I could tell he was disappointed. This was not my scene, and I feared that before the night was over he was going to wish he'd never brought me.

"Okay," he said through a forced smile.

"Here, have a seat. I just saw someone who needs me." Preston stood up and pulled his empty stool out for me. I glanced back at Cage, and he nodded for me to go on and sit down. If I wasn't going to dance, I guess he figured I might as well get comfortable.

"I thought Cage was working out on a farm all summer. Where'd he pick you up at?" Trisha asked, leaning forward on the table so I could hear her.

"He works on my daddy's farm," I explained. Her eyes grew wide, and she shifted them toward Cage.

"Let it go, Trisha. It's different." His response to her questioning gaze was curt and cold.

"Really . . . ?" Her voice trailed off as she looked back at me. The sudden scrutiny had me thinking that maybe the dance floor was a safer option.

"Where's the restroom?" I asked Trisha, needing some excuse to go take a deep breath and relax. I knew I must look as uptight as I felt.

"Come on, I'll show you," Trisha said, standing up from her stool.

"I'll be back in a minute," I said to Cage as I followed quickly behind Trisha.

Chapter Fourteen

CAGE

I hoped Trisha kept her mouth shut. I should have offered to take Eva to the restroom. The last thing I needed was for Trisha to share all my shit with Eva. I'd thought bringing her here to meet everyone would feel right. Instead I was tied up in knots. Seeing Priscilla out in the parking lot had been my warning flag. Eva didn't know the real me, and if she found out exactly how fucked up I was, she would go running for good this time.

"I gotta know, man, are you really seeing someone, like, on a regular basis?" Rock asked. "I mean, she's the damn farmer's daughter. It ain't like you can fuck her and leave her. So what the hell is going on?"

He was frowning. I couldn't figure out if it was because of

the innocence dripping off Eva or if he was worried about me screwing up my scholarship.

"I'm working on it," I snapped, wishing he'd mind his own business.

"You're working on what? Bagging her?"

My head started pounding, and both my hands balled up into fists. I leveled a glare at Rock. "It isn't like that," I hissed through my teeth.

Rock leaned back and studied me. Then he shook his head slowly and let out a low whistle. "Damn. I thought I'd never see the day."

"See the day to what?" Preston asked as he set a beer and a Coke down on the table. "Those are yours, by the way," he said, pushing the drinks toward me.

"I believe Cage has gone and actually got himself feelings for some girl other than Low," Rock drawled out in an amused tone.

Preston jerked his head around and looked back at me. "What? You're serious about the brunette? Well, shit. I was hoping you'd share."

"Don't," I growled in warning, and Preston closed his mouth before he could run off more bullshit that just pissed me off.

"*Cage!* You're here!" Amanda Hardy, Marcus's little sister, came up to the table all smiles and glassy eyes. Great. Marcus would be pissed if he knew Amanda was drinking. I'd have to call Low before I left.

"Dance with me, Cage," she demanded, taking my hand and pulling me toward the dance floor. When had Amanda become a party girl? I'd always known her to be a classic good girl.

"She's trashed," I said, looking back at Preston with a frown.

He scowled and shook his head. "Just go dance with her. At least if she's dancing with you, she's safe. I've been beating the vultures off her all damn night. I'm about ready to call Marcus. Babysitting ain't my fucking job."

I was missing something here, but I went on out to the dance floor with Amanda. She pulled me out into the middle of the floor and wrapped her arms around my neck. Then she began moving in ways her brother would kill someone over.

Yeah, I was gonna need to call Low. If she kept this shit up with other guys tonight, she'd be waking up in a stranger's condo.

"I've missed you," she slurred, then cackled with laughter as she spun around in front of me and threw her arms back around my neck.

"Last I checked, you weren't a real big fan of mine," I replied.

"Oh, no! I've always been a fan of yours." She ran a fingernail down my face and across my bottom lip. Her eyes were zoned in on my mouth. Shit.

"You're not a drinker, Amanda. What's with you tonight?" I needed to distract her because I was sure as fuck not going to let her kiss me. That was the last thing I needed. Eva was already dwelling on the fact that I'd had a threesome. If she saw some girl kissing me, I was pretty damn sure I'd lose any chance of her ever seeing me as something other than a player.

"You know what I've always wondered, Cage?" Amanda asked, leaning in to me. I took a step back and she began to wobble, so I grabbed her waist to steady her.

"What's that, Amanda?" I started scanning the crowd for someone to come to my rescue.

"What it's like to kiss the famous Cage York. Girls fall mindlessly at your feet. You must be doing something right." She leaned up on her tiptoes and I moved back fast. If she fell on her drunk ass, then she deserved it. The girl shouldn't be out alone like this.

"I won't tell Marcus," she promised, staring up at me. "We can go outside to my car. No one will see."

I glanced back toward the table. I needed Preston's help now. He was looking directly at us, and he wasn't happy.

Help me, I mouthed.

Amanda's hands were now clasped behind my neck again. "I know you want to. Bad boys like you want to do it anywhere they can."

Holy *shit*! What had gotten into her?

I was checking to see if Preston was close when I saw him stalking through the crowd. He reached us and wrapped his hands around Amanda's waist. "Come on, Amanda. I'm taking you home."

"Nooooo. You're not my daddy. Go away, Preston." She reached for me, and I stepped back again.

"He's right. You need to go home."

"But don't you want to take me outside alone?" she asked in a hurt voice.

Preston shifted his gaze to me, and the murderous glare flashing in his eyes was not something I was familiar with. The guy never got mad. What the fuck was with everyone tonight?

"Her idea. Not mine. I've got a date," I reminded him.

Preston smirked and nodded at something behind me. "Looks like you might be wrong there. She seems to be having herself a fine time without you."

Eva was dancing with some guy. Some random strange guy. I'd asked her to dance and she'd turned me down, but this dude comes out of nowhere and she dances with him?

EVA

"I still can't believe you're here. When I turned around from ordering my drink and saw you sitting over at a table, I thought I was seeing things."

Brett Cortwright was one of the closest guy friends Josh had in high school. When he'd walked up to the table, I'd been so happy to see a familiar face. Cage had gone off dancing with yet another blonde. I shouldn't have been mad at him, because he'd asked me to dance and I'd said no out of fear. All the same, I was mad. I was hurt. I was jealous.

"I'm slowly starting to get out again. Jeremy is leaving next month for LSU."

Brett frowned. "Really? You okay with that?"

Why was that everyone's immediate reaction? Did they all think I couldn't survive without him?

"I'm happy for him. It's time he got back to his life. We've both been on pause for a while now."

Brett nodded in agreement. A slower song started to play. "You up for a slow dance? I won't bite," he teased.

I'd only ever slow danced with Josh. I started to say yes, but then Brett took a step back from me. Confused, I looked up at him, and he was focused on something behind me.

"Good idea. Go on. Get the hell away from her."

Cage's angry snarl startled me, and I spun around to see him glaring at Brett. What was he doing? "*Cage!* Stop that," I demanded. "Don't go anywhere, Brett."

Cage's furious expression shifted to me. "You're on a first-name basis now? Is this what you're looking for? A preppy momma's boy with good fucking manners?"

My blood was boiling. I'd never been this mad in my life. I stalked over until I was as close to being in Cage's face as I could get.

"It isn't any of your business who I dance with. You can apologize to Brett, or I'm leaving!" I yelled.

Cage smirked, but the angry gleam still flashed in his eyes. "I ain't apologizing to anyone, sweetheart."

I wanted to scream and punch his chest and cry because he wasn't who I'd thought he was. He wasn't the sweet guy I'd gotten to know the past couple of weeks. I should've told Brett good-bye, but I couldn't. I was too close to tears. So I ran.

I heard Cage call my name as I pushed through the crowd, but I didn't look back. He'd shown his true colors tonight. I'd fallen for his act, but not again. My chest ached, and the lonely feeling I'd slowly been overcoming was seeping back in. I pushed out the first set of doors I came to and ran out into the parking lot. This wasn't where my Jeep was parked. The tears I'd tried to hold back had finally started to fall, and my vision was blurry. I hated this. I just wanted to go home. I wanted to cuddle into my covers and be safe. No more pain. No more being let down.

I started walking. I'd just walk around the building until I found my Jeep. Maybe I could find it before anyone came out here and saw me like this. I hated looking weak.

"Eva!" Cage's voice called out from behind me. I wanted to run, but I was wearing heels and walking on gravel. I'd just end up falling into a heap if I tried. Even so, I didn't have to stop. If he wanted to talk to me, then he could do it while I walked. It would be easier to ignore him that way.

"Eva." He repeated my name again as he caught up to me. I didn't turn my head to acknowledge him.

"I'm sorry. I saw you with that guy, and I snapped. I didn't think about your feelings; I just cared that he was touching you. I didn't want him touching you. I was wrong." The pleading sound to his voice was a little more powerful than I'd have thought. I stopped walking, but I kept staring straight ahead. I was afraid to look into his eyes just yet. If he was as sorry as he sounded, then his eyes would tell me and I'd melt. Damn his pretty face.

"Brett was a friend of Josh's. He wasn't some strange guy in a bar."

Cage let out a heavy sigh. "Fuuuck."

"You were dancing with some girl. I don't see how me dancing with some guy was any different."

Cage's fingers wrapped around my arm. "Please look at me, Eva."

He was really good at the begging thing. His voice even dropped to a low, sexy rumble. Dang it.

I shifted so that I was facing him. His pale-blue eyes looked desperate.

"I'm a jackass. I know that. I'm sorry. I never should have treated you that way."

"Me? What about poor Brett?"

Cage frowned. "I didn't touch him."

"But you were rude to him."

Cage gently tugged on my arm to pull me closer to him.

"The girl I was dancing with was Amanda Hardy. She's Marcus Hardy's, Low's fiancé's, little sister. She was trashed, and that is not normal for her. I danced with her because I was worried about who she might grab up if I turned her down."

So he was being kind. Not what I was expecting.

"Okay. I understand that," I replied.

"Will you come back inside?" he asked as he cupped the side of my face with his hand.

"Will you apologize to Brett?"

Cage's soft expression went hard, but for only a moment. Then the corner of his mouth tilted up. "Probably not."

"Then I'm not going back inside," I replied.

Cage's face fell. "But I never got to dance with you."

Now that Brett had broken me in to dancing in that mass of people, I was a little disappointed that I hadn't been able to dance with Cage.

"Okay, but just one dance."

Chapter Fifteen

CAGE

The tightness in my chest had finally eased by the time I got Eva back inside the doors of Live Bay. Seeing her tear-streaked face had only made the panic worse. If she'd really pushed it, I'd have come back in here and found the guy and apologized. I was ready to do whatever she wanted me to in order to get her to forgive me.

I'd taken her to the Jeep so she could get her purse and fix her face before we had come back inside. I'd also made sure to get a good long kiss out of her too. Just to feel her safely in my arms and not running away from me had been the biggest relief. The fact that she tasted like the cotton candy lip balm she'd put on was an added bonus.

I noticed a girl who I was pretty sure I'd screwed a while back making her way toward us. I really didn't want any more of my past to be exposed to Eva tonight. She'd met her quota of Cage shit. It was a miracle she hadn't insisted I take her home already. Reaching down, I took her hand and threaded her fingers through mine. The simple fact that she let me do this made me feel like one lucky son of a bitch.

I lifted our joined hands and spun her around as she giggled, then pulled her up close to me. "Mmmm . . . you smell good," I whispered in her ear as I fit her body as close as I could against mine. Her hands trailed up my chest until her left hand felt the barbell under my shirt. Smiling up at me, she ran her thumb over it before slipping both hands behind my neck.

"Is it just piercings that get you hot, or do you like tats, too? Because I got a killer one just under my boxer briefs that I'll let you feel later if you want," I teased. Her head snapped back in shock until she saw the teasing smile on my face. Her laughter was just what I needed to make better the disaster the night had been so far.

"You are such a bad boy." She tugged on the hair that brushed my collar.

"I can be real bad. You haven't seen anything yet," I murmured, bending my head so I could take a nip at the soft skin on her neck.

"I'm not sure I could keep up with you. I'm extremely inexperienced. We are on completely different planets when it comes to sexual experience." Her breathing was labored as I licked and kissed different sweet spots on her shoulder and collarbone.

"I didn't say anything about sex, Eva." I grinned before kissing her jawline. "You're the naughty one who brought up sex."

Watching her chest rise and fall quickly was making me get a little carried away. I wanted to dance, but damned if I didn't also want to get her ass back to my bed.

The groove of the music changed, and I spun her around and pressed her back up against me. I took both her hands and wrapped them around my neck. "This is a really good view," I whispered into her ear.

She had stiffened up. This was something new for her. I slid my hands down her rib cage and moved my hips against her to the beat of the music. Slowly, she began feeling the music. Her eyes closed, and I pressed my hands against her hip bones and moved her body with mine.

Her head tilted to one side, and I took advantage of her exposed neck. Forgetting the room full of people and the band playing one of my favorite songs, I enjoyed holding Eva as she let go and just went with what she felt. No thought or caution. It was beautiful to watch.

Eva thought she was the inexperienced one, but she wasn't. I was. Eva knew what it felt like to hold someone she cared for in her arms. She knew what it felt like to hurt when they hurt and to want to make them happy. She knew what it felt like to be touched and kissed by someone who wasn't a one-night stand.

Sex with Eva wouldn't be just sex for me. I'd never had that.

It would be . . . more. So much more than I'd ever imagined. Was I ready for that?

The music changed, and Eva turned back around in my arms and stood on her tiptoes to place a kiss on my lips before threading her fingers with mine. "That was fun."

I lowered my head to give her a deeper kiss. Even having that connection with her was different for me. "Yeah, it was fun," I replied after getting her taste on my lips. "You interested in meeting the band?"

She glanced up at the stage as Jackdown was announcing their break. "Yeah, sure."

"I'm warning you now, Krit is your typical lead singer. He thinks all he has to do is smile and girls will drop their panties. I'm gonna make sure he understands that you're off-limits, but he may still make suggestive comments. I'll take him outside and beat his ass if I need to."

Eva just laughed. She thought I was kidding. She'd obviously never met a lead singer before. I just hoped Krit didn't really piss me off. Depended on how high he was.

EVA

Cage led me back over to the table we'd been at earlier. There were a lot more people around it now. Another table had been pulled up beside it. The band members I'd noticed earlier were all gathering around the other table and yelling their orders to the bartender. Trisha was laughing and shoving the shirtless lead singer. He was sitting in her lap, shaking his sweaty hair on her. I was a little surprised that her badass-looking husband wasn't upset by this. Then the lead singer lifted his head, and his eyes met mine. I saw the resemblance instantly. His eyes were the exact same color and shape as Trisha's. They also had very similar mouths.

"I may beat his ass just because of the way you're looking at him," Cage growled beside me. Startled by his sudden angry tone, I turned my attention to him.

"What?"

He was snarling at the shirtless guy with long sweaty hair.

"Cage?"

He finally tore his intense expression off the lead singer and looked at me. "Yeah?"

"I was looking at him because I was surprised he was sitting in Trisha's lap like that, and then when I saw his face, I figured out the resemblance. That was all."

His frown eased. "Okay. Good."

"The convict is ba-ack," the lead singer said in a singsong voice.

"Eva, the thug in Trisha's lap is her brother, Krit. And, Krit, this is Eva. Stay the fuck away," Cage said by way of introduction.

Krit's blond eyebrows shot up, and he jumped out of his sister's lap, gawking at me. "Shiiiit. Cage York has been collared? Say it ain't so, bro. Say it ain't fuckin' so." The amazement in Krit's voice was a little disturbing. Was it really that hard for everyone to believe that Cage was on a date? With a girl he didn't want to share?

"What's this I hear?" The shirtless bass player who'd sung a couple songs leaned over on the table with a shot of something in his hand. His entire chest and arms were covered in tattoos.

"That one," Krit said, pointing toward us with the hand that held his beer. "Cage won't share her. Your ugly mug won't be basking in the advantages of Cage's pretty face tonight. He has his woman. He ain't gonna be snagging a couple to share with you."

Cage tensed up beside me. I didn't have to ask why.

"Eva, that idiot is Green. He plays bass, and he gets to sing when Krit will share the spotlight."

I'd noticed him earlier when I'd been sitting at the table. Watching someone who actually knew how to play the bass well was always intriguing to me.

"You're good. I'm impressed by the fact that you can actually pull off Flea's stuff."

Krit and Green both froze.

"You know who the bassist for the Red Hot Chili Peppers is?" Green asked me. The shock on his face made me smile.

"Yes, I do. Flea is one of the greats, in my opinion. But John Paul Jones is my all-time favorite," I replied.

Green slammed his still-full shot glass on the table, and some of it splashed over the side. "Holy shit! She knows the bassist for Led fucking Zeppelin!"

He shifted his awed look to Cage. "I'll do anything, man. Just let me have her, please?"

Cage's arm wrapped around my waist, and he pulled me closer to his side. "Not happening. Back off."

"Fuck, man, do you know how many girls I've met who don't even know what the hell a bassist is? *None!* Fucking *none!* Where'd you get her? I want one too."

Cage chuckled beside me. "Sorry, man. It's not happening."

"You could maybe go to a music school and actually meet girls who know how to play the bass. Typically the ones you pick up in bars only know how to unzip your pants," I informed him.

The entire table burst into laughter. Cage placed a kiss on the top of my head and squeezed my side.

"Okay, hell, now I want one," Krit chimed in.

"You are bringing her around more often, Cage. I like this one," Trisha said, smiling at me.

"What do you mean by 'this one'?" Green asked before draining his shot glass. "There ain't ever been one he kept more than a couple hours."

"That's enough, you two," Rock spoke up for the first time.

"I'm not in the mood to keep your asses from being strung up by Cage tonight. If he decides to shut you up, I'm gonna let him."

"He knows we're kidding." Krit shot me a cocky grin and winked.

"Fuuuck, I ain't kidding. I want her," Green said before turning to take another shot glass from a waitress.

"MATTY!" Krit called out over the crowd.

I noticed girls with too much makeup and not enough clothing hovering around us like vultures. Were they waiting on one of the band members to notice them?

A guy with really tight jeans and long hair that stuck straight up in the air sauntered up with a girl on each arm. Neither of them looked older than seventeen. I was more than positive they weren't legal.

"Please tell me you checked ID," Green moaned in annoyance.

"I trust them. They're both eighteen, aren't you, girls?"

The girls bobbed their heads in unison.

"Sure they are," Cage muttered beside me.

The new guy finally looked our way, and his focus shifted from Cage to me and back to Cage. "You already picked one for the night?"

Cage made an aggravated sound in his throat. "Eva, this is Matty, the drummer. Matty, this is Eva, my date." The warning look in Cage's eyes wasn't lost on me.

Matty's surprised expression was something I was getting used to. If it was really this crazy for Cage to date just one girl, then why was he out with me? If we slept together, would that be it? Would he be done with me? Had I kidded myself into thinking he was a nice guy? Because I knew he wasn't exactly a good guy.

"I'll be damned," Matty replied.

"Yeah, we already knew you were damned. Even before you decided to have a go with two high school freshmen," Krit drawled in an amused tone.

"I told you, they're eighteen," Matty insisted.

"We're up in two," Green interrupted them, and took one last swallow from his newest shot glass. How many had he drunk during his five-minute break?

"Bring her back," Green called out to Cage, and then winked at me.

"Sorry about him. But you did unleash some stellar knowledge of famous bassists. That's like porn for Green," Cage said with a smirk.

"They were entertaining," I assured him.

He pulled me around to face him and studied me a moment. "Want to tell me how you know about bass guitarists?"

Was I ready to share this with Cage? I'd only played my acoustic once the other night. Sharing more of Josh with Cage almost felt wrong. If Cage was just in my life for the summer, then did I want to give him that much of me? If I had imagined that there could be more for us, that had been killed tonight. Cage didn't do commitment. I was just a summer fling.

I shrugged. "I like guitars, I guess."

He didn't buy it. I could see it in his eyes, but he didn't push me either.

"You ready to go?" he asked.

"Yeah, I think I am."

Chapter Sixteen

CAGE

I hadn't said much on the drive back to my apartment. Eva was cautious. I knew this. I'd known it from day one when she'd basically called me a man whore. It was one of the things I liked about her. Up until tonight I had been making progress. She'd told me about Josh. I'd been able to hold her while she cried. I thought that had formed a bond of trust between us.

Taking her into my world had undone everything I'd worked damn hard to prove to her. If I didn't have girls throwing themselves at me and talking about our threesomes, I had my friends acting like I used girls like disposable objects. I'd wanted my friends to meet her. I'd wanted her to know me—until she got a real taste of my life. Now I wanted to get her back to the country so we could live in our little cocoon where my past wasn't there to haunt me.

"Are you mad at me?" Eva's question snapped me out of my thoughts. I lifted my eyes from the spot on the floor I'd been staring at to see Eva standing in the doorway wearing a pair of tiny pink polka-dot pajama bottoms and a matching tank top. It was the sexiest thing I'd ever seen.

"Huh?" I managed to ask through the lust haze that had settled over me. She wasn't wearing a bra. I swallowed hard as her nipples pebbled under my gaze and pressed against the thin, silky fabric.

"You didn't talk the whole way back from the bar. I thought maybe you were mad at me about something."

Mad at her? What?

I tore my eyes off her tits and focused on her worried face. "No, I'm not mad at you. I just had some stuff on my mind."

She shifted her feet and chewed on the inside of her cheek nervously.

"Come here," I invited, patting the spot beside me on the end of the bed.

She came willingly. I tried to focus on her face and on making her less nervous. But damned if the fact that those shorts barely covered up her ass wasn't distracting. She sat down beside me, fisting her hands together in her lap. I reached over and covered her hands with mine.

"Relax, Eva. I'm not mad at you. I'm frustrated with myself."

She tilted her head to the side and looked up at me. Her

silky brown locks slid over her bare shoulder. Had I ever noticed how sexy something as simple as a bare shoulder could be?

"Why are you frustrated with yourself?"

Because I'm a fuckup and now you know it.

"Tonight didn't go as well as I'd hoped. I don't have a very stellar reputation, and it seemed like everyone who knew me wanted to make sure you knew just what a sordid past I have."

Her shoulders relaxed, and she leaned over and bumped my arm with her shoulder. "You do realize that I never thought you had a stellar reputation." Her teasing tone made me smile.

"What? You didn't think I was next in line for Pope? Damn, I thought I had you fooled."

Eva laughed and pulled her legs underneath her, then turned her body so she was facing me. "Yeah, the whole DUI thing kind of clued me in."

"You think you're a funny one, don't you?" I leaned back on my elbows so I could look up at her. Also because I had a real good view of her ass now that her shorts were inched up enough to show me the bottom curve of her perfectly rounded cheeks.

"I had fun tonight. Your friends are very entertaining."

The one friend she'd had there I'd threatened. "I'm really sorry about the thing with your friend. I snapped."

A small frown puckered her brow, and then she shrugged. "You apologized for that already and I forgave you, but in the future, if you could refrain from threatening people because of me, that would be nice."

I didn't respond because that probably wouldn't happen. If she was with another guy, I would be seeing red. No use in making any promises I couldn't keep.

"I really like those pj's." I changed the subject and reached over to run my finger along the edge of the shorts. I couldn't look at her ass any longer and not at least touch it.

She shivered and pressed her lips together tightly. How innocent was she? She'd been with Josh for forever. They'd been engaged. Surely she wasn't a virgin. No guy would be able to make it through high school without getting him some. I didn't want to know what all she'd done with him. Even if the guy was dead, I couldn't handle images of some other guy touching her. Considering I couldn't even count the number of girls I'd been with, it was fucked up that I cared about her being with just one guy. But I hadn't loved one of those girls. She'd loved Josh. It made a difference. At least in my head it did.

"I want . . . I want to do things tonight. I— I mean, I want to do more than we have," she stammered, and her face flushed a bright pink. "But I'm not sure if I'm ready for, you know . . . sex."

I sat up and closed the space between us. The truth was, I wasn't sure I was ready for sex. It would be different for me this time. It scared the shit out of me. Sex and emotion had never gone together before, but it had been so long since I'd been with anyone that I wasn't sure I could stop myself if we got too carried away. I wasn't used to stopping, and I sure as hell had never been told no.

But this was Eva. I could do this for Eva.

I slid one hand around her waist and slid my other hand into her head full of hair. "We will only do what you want to do. We stop when you say stop," I whispered as I lowered my mouth to hers. She tilted her head back and met my mouth eagerly.

EVA

Even though I'd kissed Cage several times now, I still briefly lost all thought when his soft, full lips touched mine. His kisses always glided smoothly over my mouth, and he never just did the same thing. He kissed and sucked and left little licks with a flick of his tongue. He really liked sucking on my bottom lip, and he spent a lot of time tasting me. Or at least, that's what it felt like. He kissed a trail across my jaw and down my neck. I wanted him to go farther. As he stopped to tease the curve of my neck, I had to clench my teeth to keep from begging him to keep going down. A whimper escaped me and I probably should have been embarrassed, but he began traveling closer to the tops of my breasts, so instead I was thankful. Anything to get him moving. My breasts already knew what was coming. They were tingling.

His hands grazed my stomach, startling me. He lifted his

head to look up at me when I gasped. He didn't ask, but I could see the question in his eyes. I nodded, and he eased the pajama top up and over my chest, and I lifted my arms so he could take it the rest of the way off.

The way he stared hungrily at my naked breasts only caused the tingling to intensify. I wanted his shirt off. I wanted to feel his warm skin against mine.

Before he could distract me with his mouth, I reached for his shirt and pulled it up, and he raised his hands for me so I could take it off easily. The nipple ring I'd felt under his shirt earlier only excited me more. I'd started to lean forward when Cage leaned up over me and forced me to lie back as he covered my body with his.

"As much as I like seeing your little tongue licking my nipple, I want to taste first this time." His voice was low and raspy.

I ran my hands through his hair as he lowered his mouth to my breast and pulled one of my nipples into his mouth. With each pull from his mouth, I lost more and more conscious thought. The heat between my legs was becoming uncomfortable. I rubbed my legs together, needing relief. Cage ran a hand down my stomach and slipped his fingers inside the top of my shorts. He slid his fingers back and forth, only causing my need to grow hotter. I was so close to pleading with him to do more. He stopped playing with my shorts, and his hand moved away. My small cry of frustration only made him smile.

He moved his weight to one side, and then his hand was on my knee, opening one of my legs as his hand eased its way up the sensitive skin of my thigh until his thumb touched the edge of my panties. I could hear my own panting breaths as I waited for something.

When he ran a finger along the lace around my leg, I broke down. "Please," I begged. His head lifted, and his eyes met mine. I stared into his heavily lidded blue eyes as his finger slipped underneath the lace and slid along the wet heat of my folds.

"Ohgod." I gasped, closing my eyes as the ecstasy from his touch controlled me. Cage's warm breath tickled my bare stomach as his finger slid easily inside me. I was on the edge of bursting into a million pieces. The need to beg him was still there.

He moved up my body, kissing each nipple and licking a trail between my cleavage before moving back up my neck. His finger stayed firmly inside me. Just barely.

"I'm about to pump this tight little hole with my finger," he said in a ragged voice. Each hot breath against my ear gave me chills.

"Okay," I choked out.

His finger slowly eased out and back in, and I thought I was going to die from pleasure.

"Does that feel good, baby?" he asked, pressing a kiss beside my ear.

"Mmmm-hmmm," I managed to moan.

He ran the tip of his nose against the side of my face. "You're so wet. So hot," he murmured into my hair.

I liked him talking to me while he touched me. Hearing the effect it was having on him in his voice only made everything better.

"Cage," I whimpered as he started pumping in and out faster.

"Yeah, sweetheart?" he asked while kissing back down my neck.

"I want you to take off your jeans," I managed to croak out.

His hand stopped moving, and he lifted his head and looked at me. "Why?"

"I want to feel more of you against me," I whispered.

Cage dropped his head and took a deep breath. He didn't move for several seconds. Finally he looked back up at me with a tortured expression on his face. "I need to leave on my underwear. I can't . . . I need there to be a barrier."

I nodded in agreement. When he slipped his hand out of my panties, I wanted to protest. But I'd been the one to ask him to strip. He couldn't exactly do that with one finger inside me.

He stood up and slowly unbuttoned his jeans. He was either teasing me or giving me time to change my mind. Once he had them undone, his gaze locked with mine and I smiled. Then Cage York slipped his jeans off his hips and let them fall to the floor, where he stepped out of them. The white boxer briefs he was wearing didn't leave a lot to the imagination.

I watched his beautiful body as he crawled back over me,

and I let my legs fall open so that his hardness would press directly on the source of my heat.

The second he shifted on top of me, I cried out.

"Fuck, Eva." He took a shaky breath and held himself still over me. I didn't want him still. Lifting my hips, I rubbed against him, and his arms trembled.

"I don't want to lose control with you, Eva." His voice sounded desperate.

"It's okay." I ran my hands through his hair and lifted my hips again. We still had too many layers of fabric between us. I wanted my shorts off.

"I want inside you. 'S not okay," he replied through gritted teeth.

I moved my hands down to my shorts and started pushing them down. Cage groaned loudly as I shimmied my shorts down until they were at my ankles and I could kick them off. Now we only had his underwear and the lace of my panties between us.

"Kiss me," I said, lifting my head to meet his lips. The hunger in his kiss was exciting. Small growls escaped him as he explored my mouth like a man starving.

Slowly, he lowered himself down until we were pressed so tightly together that all I had to do was rock my hips to get some friction.

Cage tore his mouth off mine just before he began rocking his hips against me. That was so much better.

"Yes, please," I encouraged him.

His arms bulged on each side of me as he held himself up so he could look down at me. I ran my hands up his chest and found the barbell I loved so much.

"AH!" he cried out as I gently tugged on it. His obvious pleasure made mine increase. I lifted my hips in sync with him, and he let out a low groan, closing his eyes tighter.

"I want inside, Eva. I want inside so damn bad."

The desperation in his face and the need in his voice sent me over the edge. My world combusted, and I cried out as everything inside me ignited into flames.

Chapter Seventeen

CAGE

Eva's head was thrown back, and her long dark curls were fanned out over the pillow as she cried out my name. The tremors that coursed through her body only caused her to press harder against my ready-to-explode dick.

Somehow I'd managed to keep from ripping her panties off and shoving my briefs down so I could bury myself inside her and find relief. This was not a position I'd ever been in, and it was painful as shit.

Her long lashes fluttered open slowly as her body began to relax underneath me. A small smile played on her lips, and I suddenly felt like a damn rock star. I might be harder than fucking cement, but I'd made her feel damn good. That put a smile on my face.

"Wow," she said breathlessly. Her eyelids were droopy. She'd sleep good tonight. I wouldn't mind tucking her in like this every night.

"You're gorgeous, but when you come it's beautiful," I whispered, brushing the hair out of her face.

"You sure know the right things to say to a girl," she said in a low, raspy voice.

Part of me wanted to get angry at her flippant assumption, but I knew she only knew what she'd been told.

"Make no mistake. I've never stayed around long enough to say thanks after I get off. Much less to tell a girl that she is beautiful when she comes. I've never cared to watch anyone else."

A small O formed on her red, swollen lips. I bent down and pressed a kiss to them, then lifted myself up off her. I needed to go finish this off in the bathroom. There was no way I'd get any sleep like this.

"Where are you going?" she asked sleepily as I stood up.

"I got some business to take care of. I'll be back in a few minutes." I winked and headed for the bathroom.

Stepping inside, I studied the shower and tried to decide if I should just take a cold shower or if I was so far gone I needed to grab the baby oil.

"Cage?" Eva called out.

"Yeah?"

"Can I come in?"

Fuck. Did she really not realize I'd come in here to beat off?

The door opened and she stepped inside. She'd put her tank top back on, but she was still wearing those lacy panties I knew for a fact were soaked. My cock throbbed harder just thinking about it.

"Can I do it?" she asked nervously.

"Do what?"

She walked over to stand in front of me and slid her hand down over my erection from hell.

"I want to make it better," she whispered.

I dropped my attention from her face to her hand on my cock. She moved it up, gently squeezing, and my knees buckled. Oh fuck, yeah.

"Yeah," I croaked out, and leaned back against the wall for support.

She lightly trailed her fingernail down my chest before taking the waistband of my boxers and pushing them down. I stared down in fascination as she knelt in front of me until my underwear was on the floor. I stepped out of them, and she moved them away before standing back up and placing a kiss on my chest.

If she kept this up, I was going to erupt without her touching me.

"Do you have lotion?" she asked, looking up at me through her eyelashes.

"Baby oil. Bottom drawer."

She turned and found the bottle that was rarely used and poured some into both her hands and warmed it up. I watched her with rapt fascination and came real close to begging.

She turned back to me, and both her slippery, warm hands covered me and began sliding up and down my swollen dick.

"Holy shit," I groaned, letting my head fall back on the wall.

Her warm mouth covered my pierced nipple, and I felt my knees start to give out again. I wasn't going to last long.

Opening my eyes, I watched as Eva's tongue flicked my nipple and pulled it every few licks to suck on it. When she moved back to stare down at her hands, I followed her gaze. The sight of both her small hands sliding up and down my cock sent me over the edge.

"Fuck, I'm gonna come. Move," I ordered, standing up. She didn't move. Instead she pressed me up against the wall with her small body, and her grip tightened. I exploded in her hands.

"Ahhhhhh!" I cried out as she kept slowly pumping me until there was no more left. I stared down at the mess she was determined to participate in.

I couldn't believe she'd just done that. Hell, I couldn't believe I'd just let her. When was the last time I'd been jacked off by a girl? Junior high? Probably. But damn if that wasn't the hottest thing I'd ever seen. Would everything with Eva be like this? Was it all going to be so much . . . more?

"Oh." She breathed, smiling up at me. "I liked that."

Laughing, I reached for the nearest towel and started cleaning her up first.

"Not as much as I did," I replied.

"Yeah, probably not. You look like you enjoyed it quite a bit," she teased as I wiped off her hands.

EVA

Cage was wrapped around me when I opened my eyes the next morning. His arm held me up tightly against his chest, and his leg was between mine. I snuggled closer. This was nice. I'd never slept with a guy before. Except for the night I'd gotten drunk and slept with Cage in the barn.

Last night had been amazing. I forgot how much I missed being close to someone that way. Josh and I had never had sex, but we'd messed around. Although we'd never rubbed against each other until I came, I had helped him get off many times when our kissing and touching had gotten him all worked up. He'd never come on my hands. He always pulled away and covered himself first. With Cage I'd wanted more. Maybe it was because I was older now. I wanted things I'd never wanted back then.

If it wasn't for the fact that I was just one of many for Cage, I would have been willing to go all the way. My body had sure wanted to, and his desperate declaration about wanting to be inside me had been hard to resist. However, I couldn't let what was happening between us become too important. Summer would end and he would leave. I needed to look at our time together as a time of healing. I could enjoy it while it lasted.

"Mmmmmm, you feel good," Cage whispered into my ear in a husky voice.

His hand trailed down to tickle my stomach, and I giggled and squirmed.

"No squirming," he warned, and put some space between his erection and my bottom.

"Okay, fine. I'll be good." I rolled over and stared up at him. He propped his head up with his hand and grinned wickedly down at me.

"Just so you know, I felt you up in your sleep," he admitted.

"What?" I asked, sitting up some.

"I'm teasing. Well, maybe not completely. I did slip my hand under your top and play with those incredible tits of yours. But you enjoyed it. I was there."

Laughing, I threw my pillow at his head and crawled out of bed.

"Hey! Where you going?"

I threw my hair over my shoulder and glanced back at him. "I'm starving. I'm going to see if there is food to eat in this place."

Cage groaned. "Food. I forgot to get food."

He swung his legs off the bed and stood up, then stretched. Every tanned muscle in his body flexed and bulged. Suddenly food no longer seemed important.

He finished and caught me gawking. "I normally charge for that show, but you get it for free." He winked and grabbed a pair of jeans out of his closet.

I was starting to suggest he just leave the jeans off and do that stretchy thing again when a knock at the door interrupted me.

Who would be here this early? I stepped back into the room and went over to my bag to find some clothes.

Cage didn't bother with a shirt. His jeans hung deliciously on his hips and showcased the two dimples in his lower back. I wanted to lick those next time.

"It's probably Low," he said, heading out the bedroom door and closing it behind him so I could get dressed.

I wasn't sure I wanted to officially meet Low now that I knew who she was. I pulled out the short yellow sundress I'd brought and slipped it on. I'd left my toiletry bag in Cage's bathroom last night. My hair and teeth both needed a brush.

I tried hard to look presentable without going to the trouble of putting on makeup. I pulled my hair over my shoulder and put a ponytail holder in it to keep it from going wild. I would need a shower before we went anywhere.

When I opened the door and stepped into the kitchen, the smell of coffee hit my nose. Thank God.

"There she is," Cage said, smiling at me. He was sitting on the counter with a cup of coffee in his hand. Still shirtless and looking too beautiful for his own good. "Low brought food." He jumped down off the counter and came over to me.

"Eva, you remember Low. She committed the great offense of changing my sheets." Cage was grinning like a little boy at his attempt to be funny.

Low laughed, and it sounded almost musical. "Leave her alone, Cage. It isn't nice to tease females. You know better," she scolded him.

Low held up two large brown paper bags. "I knew he wouldn't have any food here, and I hated for y'all to wake up hungry. So I brought biscuits, sausage, eggs, and doughnuts if you prefer sweets for breakfast."

My stomach rumbled. I put a hand over it, and Cage chuckled. "Come on, girl, I'll feed you."

Cage took the bags from Low and began opening them and getting down plates from the cabinet. I turned my attention to Low. "I'm really sorry about how rude I was when we met. I don't know why I acted so ridiculous over sheets and a towel...." I trailed off, hoping she accepted my moment of stupidity.

Low smiled and cut her eyes over to Cage. "Don't worry about it. I completely understand. I shouldn't have just intruded."

Trying to explain myself would only prove to be embarrassing, so I decided to let it go. Maybe she'd just forget about it eventually.

"Your breakfast is served," Cage said, bringing me a plate of food. "Go sit down and I'll pour you coffee."

"Thank you," I replied. He'd put some of everything on my plate. I wasn't about to complain. I was starving.

"Coffee with two creams and a sugar, right?" he said as he walked toward the coffeepot.

I started to reply and stopped. How did he know that? We'd never had coffee together.

When I didn't reply, he glanced back at me. He saw the question in my eyes, and his cocky smirk tugged at his lips.

"You told Jeremy once what you wanted in your coffee while you were sitting in the rocking chair on the front porch. He was inside, so you called it out. I was unloading the truck and I heard you," he explained.

Wow.

"Oh," I replied, feeling Low's eyes on me. She was watching us closely.

"So, you met everyone last night? Are you terrified now?" Low asked in a chipper tone as I sat down at the table across from her.

"They were nice. Very entertaining."

Cage laughed. "That's her way of saying my friends are all a bunch of freaks."

"That is not true. I really did like them."

Cage walked over and set a cup of coffee down beside my plate, then placed a kiss on my head before going back to fix himself something to eat. The curiosity in Low's face almost made me laugh. Did she not know this man better than anyone else? Surely she wasn't shocked by anything he said or did.

"When do y'all have to go back today?" Low asked.

I had just taken a bite of my eggs and couldn't answer her.

"I figure we'll head out about five or so. I want to get her back before her dad gets home. And I need to check the cows before I get in bed."

Low turned her curious gaze off me and shifted it to Cage. I didn't need to look up to know they were having a silent conversation. I used to have those with Josh. I understood them. My chest ached a little at the thought of never having that again. But it didn't hurt nearly as badly as it used to. I was getting better. Maybe someday I would actually be able to move on.

Cage cleared his throat, and I knew that he was letting Low know that their silent conversation was over. Another signal I'd used with Josh.

"Well, what are y'all planning on doing today?" Low asked.

I glanced up from my plate and looked to Cage. I had no idea what all he wanted to do today.

"I thought we'd spend a few hours on the beach, and that's about as far as I've gotten with plans," Cage replied.

"That sounds like fun." Low started to say more, but her phone began ringing. She glanced down at it and frowned.

"Who is it?" Cage asked, watching her carefully.

Low sighed and stood up. "It's my sister."

Cage scowled. "Want me to get rid of her?"

Low shook her head and headed into the other room before I heard her say, "Hello?"

Cage was watching the door, standing in a strange, protective stance. It almost looked like he was ready to snatch the phone out of her hand if her sister said anything to upset her.

"Is her relationship with her sister that bad?" I asked, wanting him to relax. He turned his head toward me, and his shoulders eased when our eyes met. "Yeah. Her sister's a bitch. She's put Low through hell."

But Low had obviously had a very loyal Cage to fend off the bullies in her life. "If you need to go check on her, it's okay."

He studied me a minute, and then a pleased smile came over his face. "If she needs me, she'll come get me. I'd rather sit in here with you and enjoy my breakfast."

Chapter Eighteen

CAGE

Eva had dozed off while we lay out under a large beach umbrella and watched the waves. I'd been worried about the parts of her that weren't completely covered by the shade, and I'd woken her up rubbing lotion on her feet.

Both those big blue eyes of hers watched me intently as I went from rubbing lotion on her feet to massaging them. "Mmmm, that's nice. I hope you aren't expecting a tip," she said in a sleepy voice.

"I don't work for free."

"I'm afraid to ask what form of payment you accept."

I could think of a few different things to say, but I decided to be careful with my words. Eva had seen and heard enough stuff last night, as far as I was concerned. I didn't want her to think I was being serious.

"Are you getting hungry?" I'd decided to change the subject.

She sat up a little straighter and gave me a shy smile. "Yeah, kinda."

I picked her foot up from its resting spot on my leg and laid it back down on the chair. "Let's go eat," I replied, holding a hand out to pull her up.

"Are we going back inside? Do I need to gather our things up?"

"No, we can leave it all right here. It won't get touched. I know a guy," I assured her.

A small frown puckered her lips. I decided, what the hell. If she was going to do sexy shit like that with her lips, I was going to react the way I wanted.

I bent my head and pressed my lips firmly against hers before pulling that sweet bottom lip of hers into my mouth. Her hands grabbed me, and she made a small surprised gasp. Smiling, I pulled back and winked at her before reaching down to take her hand.

"What was that for?" she asked a little breathlessly.

"You do sexy little frowns and pucker those lips of yours, and I'm not gonna be able to ignore that."

A slow smile spread across her whole her face, and she licked her lips. "Oh."

I led us over toward the Beach Shack, which was a walk-up seafood po'boy place. They also had some of the best homemade fries I'd ever eaten.

"Cage, my day just got a whole lot brighter." Rock's cousin Jess called out as she strutted toward us in an American flag string bikini. Jess was trouble. I'd made the mistake of messing around with her one night just to get her off Marcus Hardy because she was upsetting Low. Jess did not understand a no-strings-attached fuck. Rock and I had come to blows over it. After a few solid punches from each of us, we'd both felt better and decided to let it go. It wasn't like Rock didn't know Jess was an easy lay.

"Jess," I replied, threading my fingers through Eva's. You never could tell what Jess would pull.

"I heard you were shipped off to the country for being a bad boy."

Jess walked up to me and leaned in to kiss my cheek.

I moved my head back away from her lips. "Yeah. I'm off on Sundays."

Jess didn't like being snubbed. She was a major brat when things didn't go her way.

"You need to call me so we can catch up when you get back next Sunday. I miss you." She dropped her voice to a whisper, like she was sharing a secret between the two of us.

"That ain't gonna happen, Jess. I don't intend to get in another tie-up with Rock over you." *Also, you're a crazy bitch.*

Jess reached up and ran her fingernail down my arm. "I promise not to tell him."

I let go of Eva's hand and slipped my arm around her waist. "Jess, this is Eva. Eva, this is Rock's cousin Jess."

Eva seemed tense, and I hated that it was my fault she felt uncomfortable. Would I ever be able to take her anywhere and not have some chick I'd banged show up? This sucked.

I brushed my lips against her temple. She eased some in my arms and leaned in to me. That was better.

"So are you, like, in a relationship?" Jess asked incredulously.

How the hell did I answer this question? Eva wasn't some random girl I'd picked up for today's entertainment. But we weren't in an actual relationship, either.

"We're dating," Eva piped up.

Jess scowled. "Cage doesn't date."

I opened my mouth to say something to stop Jess from going on and on about my bad-boy code of ethics.

"Maybe he doesn't date you, but he is definitely dating me," Eva responded before I could say anything.

The heated annoyance of Jess's gaze was directed my way. I could feel it, but I couldn't take my eyes off Eva. She'd handled the situation herself, and the ridiculous grin on my face couldn't be helped. Damn, she was sexy when she was saucy.

Eva tilted her head back to look up at me, and I bent down and kissed the pleased smirk on her face.

"Unbelievable," Jess replied in disbelief.

"Yeah, she is," I replied, winking at Eva.

"Y'all have fun with that," Jess said sarcastically before finally stalking off.

Packing up and heading back to the farm, where she would be away from me most of the day, wasn't appealing. I wanted to keep her here with me. Last night might have started out badly, but it had taken a major turn for fucking amazing.

I threw our bags in the Jeep and headed back upstairs to help Eva, who was determined to clean up before we left.

The strumming of guitar strings met my ears when I opened the door to the apartment. A soft voice joined the song. Eva could play the guitar? I closed the door quietly behind me. It wasn't a song I was familiar with, but I knew enough about playing the guitar to know that what she was playing wasn't easy. I could play a few songs, but my talent ended there. The acoustic guitar she'd obviously found in the corner of my room was one I'd won in a bet. Krit had been pissed when he'd had to give it up. But I'd wanted a guitar, so I wasn't about to let his sorry ass out of the bet.

The smooth sound of her voice had a country feel to it, but not entirely. Eva was musically talented. There was no doubt about it. If Krit heard her, he'd have a damn orgasm. I didn't want her to see me and stop, but I couldn't keep myself from getting as close to the bedroom door as possible. I wanted to see her like this.

Her head was bent, and the curtain of her hair kept me from seeing her face. The emotion in her voice spoke to me more than any visual. Leaning against the door frame, I crossed my arms and watched her hands fly over the strings. There was no mistake. She simply didn't miss a chord. Her voice was so low I couldn't make out the words, but the ones I did hear tore at my soul.

Once the song came to an end, she lifted her head and let out a long, heavy sigh. "That's only the second time I've picked up a guitar since Josh's death," she said aloud, then turned her head to look at me. The smile on her face wasn't sad as I'd been expecting. She was happy. She had recovered something else Josh's death had taken from her.

"How long have you played?" I asked.

"Since I was five. The guitar has always fascinated me. Most musical instruments do, but the only one I've ever learned to play is the guitar. I've always wanted to play the piano, but my momma played the piano and seeing one just upsets Daddy. So I never asked for one or expressed interest in it."

I was getting a piano. It would be here the next time she came home with me. "You are amazing," I said, and walked over to sit beside her. "Will you play another one? I want to hear your voice this time."

She ducked her head and blushed. "I can't. I knew you were back there, but I couldn't see you. If you are where I can see you, I won't be able to play. You'll make me nervous."

"Hmmm." I slid my hand inside the warmth of her thighs. "What if I bribed you?"

She giggled and shook her head. "No amount of kisses can get me to sing with you looking at me. I can't. Maybe one day, but I just can't right now."

"Are you sure about that?" I asked as I leaned in and pressed a kiss to the corner of her mouth.

"Yes," she said in breathless voice.

"Mmmm . . . I don't mind trying anyway," I replied, kissing the other corner of her mouth.

"Okay."

I took the guitar out of her lap and laid it on the bed beside her before pulling her into my lap. Burying my hands in her hair, I devoured her lips.

EVA

Cage: What are you wearing?

I laughed as I read the text Cage had just sent me. He'd made sure to get my cell phone number before we got home Sunday night.

Me: Nothing.

Smiling, I waited for him to respond.

Cage: Fuck. The lake, now.

I covered my mouth to keep from laughing out loud. Daddy was in the house somewhere. I hadn't seen him since dinner.

Me: You know I can't. Daddy's still awake.
Cage: The barn, then?

I walked over to the window and stared out into the dark to see the single light on in the back of the barn.

Me: Bad idea too.
Cage: I disagree.
Me: You would. Good night.
Cage: It could be better.

The grin on my face seemed to be permanently there lately. Daddy even noticed it earlier during dinner. I wanted to tell him all about Cage, but I'd never be able to do that. He would never accept Cage, and he'd probably fire him. I didn't want to be the cause of Cage losing his scholarship. Besides, he'd be leaving in a little over a month. The summer would end, and our time together would be just a memory. I was having to remind myself of that more and more. Getting attached to Cage was bad. He had been the key to my healing. He'd forced me to get over things. No one had pushed me before him. I'd always cherish him for that.

Flopping down on the bed, the happiness I'd felt suddenly vanished. I didn't like facing the facts about Cage. And as sweet as Low was, I hated that she would never have to lose him. He'd always be there when she needed him. I envied that.

A knock on my door broke into my melancholy thoughts. "Eva girl, you awake?" Daddy called out.

"Yeah, come on in," I replied.

He eased the door open and stepped inside. He always looked so out of place in my room. He rarely stepped foot in it.

"I wanted to talk to you about something," he said, crossing his arms over his wide chest.

"Okay." I hated it when he started our talks like this. It normally meant I wasn't going to like what would follow.

"Jeremy will be leaving soon for school. Before he gets gone, I want to have him and his parents over for dinner. He's helped you every step of the way to get through everything, and they're like family, even though things turned out like they did. . . ."

I hadn't thought of that, but Daddy was right. We needed to have them over for dinner. They'd had us over so many times over the years.

"Good idea. I'll call in the morning and set things up."

Daddy nodded. "All right, then. Well, good night."

"Good night."

The invisible fairy was no more. I made sure Cage was nearby when I took him lemonade, an ice towel, and a snack. I also took these things out every chance I got instead of just a couple of times a day.

Once I knew Daddy had gone into town, I took a big slice of the chocolate cake I'd made for dinner with the Beasleys tonight out of the fridge and grabbed the other things I knew Cage needed. Watching his back as he picked up hay bales and threw them over the fence was mouthwatering. I sat down on the tailgate and decided to enjoy the show for a few minutes. He'd see me soon enough.

The sweat glistened on his back as the sun beat down on him. His work jeans fit low on his hips, giving me a perfect view of his back dimples and the very top of his boxer briefs. He bent over to grab a hay bale and stopped. He stood up and glanced back over his shoulder. When his eyes locked with mine, a wicked grin touched his lips.

"You see somethin' ya want, baby?"

"Maybe. I'm checking things out. Seeing if I'm interested," I shot back with my own evil grin.

Both of his dark eyebrows shot up, and he turned completely around, giving me a view of his sweaty chest. Oh my. That never got old.

"I see something I want," he drawled as he came toward me. My heartbeat started that silly fluttery thing it did when he got near me.

"You do?" I asked as he stopped in front of me and leaned in.

"Hell yeah, I do," he murmured. "I love chocolate."

What? My excitement turned to confusion. His arm reached out beside me and took the piece of chocolate cake I'd brought him.

"You're a tease." I pouted. He moved to take a seat beside me.

"Me? You're the one who comes strutting out here in a pair of tiny shorts and screwing up my work by ogling me. Hell, girl. You think a man can work when he knows you're looking at him like you want a taste?"

Warm pleasure from his words spread through me. He took a bite of the cake, then closed his eyes and made a low groan in his throat. Oh my.

"Damn, baby, that's good."

Yeah, it was good. The way his jaw muscles flexed as he chewed and his throat moved as he swallowed. It was real good.

"Eva," Cage said, jerking my attention off his very nice, thick, muscular neck.

"Hmmm?" I replied.

"If I'm gonna eat this cake, then you need to talk and stop looking at me like that. You keep that shit up, and I'm gonna be eating you, and to hell with who catches us."

I couldn't help it. I giggled.

"Don't laugh. That wasn't a joke," he scolded, cocking an eyebrow at me before taking another bite of cake.

I forced my eyes away from him altogether. It had been two days since we'd been able to do any kind of touching. I was getting worked up very easily.

"You got company," Cage said, standing up and moving away from me.

Company? Who? I jumped down and turned to look up at the driveway. My stomach dropped. I knew that car. Had she seen us? I had to get away from Cage.

"I gotta go," I said without looking back at him. I didn't want him to see the worry in my eyes. If I explained it to him, he'd never understand. I wasn't sure I could explain it. I just didn't want Elaine Beasley catching me with someone like Cage. She'd be so disappointed.

Rushing back up the small hill toward the house, I silently prayed that she hadn't been looking out at the cow pasture when she'd driven up.

Elaine had already gotten out of her Lincoln Town Car and was headed my way. The kind smile on her face reminded me of so much. She'd been the only mom I could remember. I was so young when I'd lost my mom. Elaine had been the stand-in while I was growing up. When I had needed a mom, Josh had always taken me to his.

"Hello, Eva," she said, holding her arms out for a hug. I went willingly. I always felt safe when Elaine hugged me. She smelled like springtime and cookies.

"Mrs. Elaine, it's so good to see you," I replied, hugging her before stepping back.

"Only because you haven't been over to visit in a couple of weeks. Just because Jeremy is moving off doesn't mean you can't come visit me."

Guilt settled in my gut. I hadn't been to see her since the day I'd started lusting over Cage York. Being in Josh's house made the fun I was having with Cage seem tainted and wrong. I didn't want to feel that way. So I'd stayed away.

She reached down and picked up my bare left hand. "Jeremy told me you finally took it off. I want you to know I'm glad. I loved him too, Eva, but sweetie, it was time to put the ring away." Her voice was gentle and motherly. It was her son I'd been letting go of when I'd taken the ring off, but she was happy about it. How?

"There are still days I want to go grab it and put it back on," I admitted.

"I know. There are days when I want to go clean his room and pull back his bed like he's coming home to get in it." The emotion in her voice tore at me. God, the pain was still there.

She shifted her gaze over my shoulder toward the barn. I saw the small, concerned pinch in her expression. "Eva, is that the boy your uncle sent here to work off some trouble he'd gotten into?"

She'd seen us.

"Yes, ma'am," I choked out. I didn't want to admit this to her, but what else could I do? She'd seen me sitting on that tailgate, all smiles, when she'd pulled up. What was she thinking? Did she think I was completely disrespecting Josh by spending time with someone who wasn't as good and moral as he had been?

"You know I love you like a daughter. You are just as much mine as Josh and Jeremy. I've always worried over you and prayed over you just like I did my boys. I still do. Josh loved you so much. You were his world from the time he was just a boy. He wanted you to have the wonderful life the two of you had planned out. But, sweetie, I can tell you that Josh would never have wanted you spending time with that boy." She nodded in the direction of the barn. "He isn't worthy of you. Josh would want you to find someone who was good and stable. Someone who could take care of you and stand by you through all life's twists and turns." Her cold hand reached out and took mine in hers with a gentle squeeze. "You deserve much better than being some little fling for a guy like that one. Don't let your sorrow and pain send you off on a road that you can't get back from."

My chest felt so heavy. Guilt. Pain. Sorrow. Loss. It all swirled together, making it hard for me to take deep breaths. Was she right? Was I throwing Josh's memory away because

Cage York had an amazing body and a sexy smile? Had I become that shallow? Oh, God. Tears stung my eyes, and Elaine pulled me back into a hug.

"I didn't mean to upset you, sweetie," she continued. "Sometimes a momma needs to help us find the right path when we veer off. That's all." She smoothed down my hair as she reassured me. "Now let's talk about other things. More positive things. Like what your plans are now that you've decided to drive that nice little Jeep again and start living your life. I want to hear all about it. You are going back to college, aren't you? I mean, you can't stay here and keep going to the community college. You're too smart for this place, Eva. Oh, and the guitar. Your daddy told me he came home to you playing the other day. I'm so proud of you."

I followed Elaine into the house, but I didn't feel like talking about any of those things. I wanted to go hide in my room and cry. If wanting to be with Cage was so bad, why did it hurt to be told it was wrong? He was the reason I was moving on. Didn't that count for something?

Chapter Nineteen

CAGE

I'd sent Eva two texts and called her once. She still hadn't responded. The invisible fairy was back, but she wasn't bringing the extra treats like the chocolate cake. All I got was a thermos of water and an ice towel. Something was fucked up.

I couldn't go looking for her and demand she talk to me. Her dad would have my ass thrown off the property. I'd lose my scholarship and I wouldn't have Eva. What the hell could I do? She wouldn't talk to me. Our last conversation had been when she'd brought me the chocolate cake. The only thing I could come up with was that something had happened with the lady who had come by and she was busy with that. Even still, why the fuck wouldn't she answer my texts?

I needed to go talk to Wilson anyway. Low could come get

me tonight as easily as tomorrow for my day off. I didn't have any responsibilities between now and tomorrow morning. As much as I didn't want to leave with Eva giving me the silent treatment, staying here would just drive me crazy. I pulled a clean shirt on, then picked up my bag and threw a few things in it.

Wilson should be inside by this time. Maybe Eva would answer the door. I'd be able to see her face even if we couldn't talk.

I headed up to the house.

The lights were all on, which was odd. Even the outside floodlights were on, illuminating the yard. The driveway was also full. Were they having a party?

I paused at the door as laughter and several voices drifted outside.

The door swung open, and Jeremy stood smiling at me. "Hey, man. What's up?"

"I need to talk to Wilson," I explained, looking past Jeremy for any sign of Eva.

"Come on in. He's at the table with the family."

The family? Whose family?

Jeremy led me inside and through a small foyer. I couldn't help but pause several times to study pictures on the wall of Eva when she was younger. She'd been beautiful her entire life. Pigtails had also been her favorite hairstyle for a really long time.

"She was ten in that one. Just gotten braces and was really upset about it. Her dad couldn't get her to smile, so he called over to the house and got me and Josh to come over. When we got there, Eva was perched on that swing with unshed tears in her eyes and an angry scowl on her face. Josh stood behind the photographer and started telling her knock-knock jokes and making funny faces."

Her head was tilted to the side, and she looked like she'd just finished giggling. My heart tugged, thinking about all the memories she had like this one reminding her daily of what she'd lost.

Jeremy started walking again, and I followed him toward the large arched entryway, where the sounds of voices and laughter were pouring out. Whoever was in there, they were having a really good time.

Jeremy stepped in in front of me. "Mom, Dad, Chad, this is Cage York. He's working for Wilson this summer. Cage, this is my family. Chad's my cousin from Louisiana I told you about, who I'm going to be rooming with."

I hadn't expected a full introduction. Apparently, neither had they. I didn't focus on any one person. When my eyes swept over the table, I recognized Jeremy's mother as the lady who had come by the other day. Fear festered at what her arrival could have meant. She was Josh's mother too. I didn't like where my mind was going with that one.

When my gaze found Eva, she wasn't looking at me. Her head was down, and she was fiddling nervously with her napkin. Fuck.

"Cage? Is there a problem?" Wilson asked.

I forced myself to look at Wilson instead of his daughter.

"I didn't mean to interrupt your dinner. I just needed to ask you if it was all right if my ride came and got me tonight."

Wilson shrugged and nodded. "I don't see why not. Sure, boy, go on. I'll see you Monday morning."

"Thanks," I replied, and swung my eyes back to Eva. She still hadn't lifted her head. I didn't want to leave like this. "It was, uh, nice to meet y'all." I didn't wait for a response. I turned and made my way back to the door. I needed to get some fresh air and try real hard to get control of the panic settling in my chest.

The screen door slammed behind me, but I didn't flinch. I just kept walking. Reaching into my pocket, I texted Low to come and get me tonight.

She'd be at least an hour. Instead of going back to the closed-in space of my makeshift bedroom, I headed down to sit on the swing under the biggest oak tree on the property. I rarely saw anyone out here. It was dark, and I could stay hidden while I gathered my thoughts.

Josh's mother had come for a visit, and Eva hadn't spoken to me since. What had been said? Had Eva seen her and realized what she was stepping down from? Josh had the nice, all-American family. I, on the other hand, just had Low. My momma hadn't made me meals and washed my clothes. Hell, my momma hadn't even taken me to the doctor when I was sick. My half-sister and I hardly ever spoke. The last I heard, she'd been busted in a meth lab with her latest boyfriend and gone to prison.

Yeah, I had one fucking fantastic family to introduce Eva to. If she thought I wasn't worthy now, without knowing all that messed-up shit, then I didn't stand a chance.

I dropped my head into my hands. Why had I let myself care? Why had I decided to fucking care about someone who was so out of my damn reach? Girls like Eva didn't want to keep me. They wanted to play with me for a while, then go find the boy their parents would approve of. I wasn't the keeping kind. I'd learned at a young age that women didn't keep me. When a guy's momma don't want him, why the fuck should anyone else? Something was wrong with me. Always had been. When I'd found Low, I'd held on to her and decided that since she was the only girl who wanted to keep me, then she would be the one I spent forever with. I knew she'd never leave me. My fuckups would never send her running away. Then she'd found Marcus, and he'd loved her in a way I never would. As much as I loved her, I couldn't love her the way it would take to be faithful.

Then came Eva. She'd shown me I could want only one woman and be damned happy about it. Too bad that just like the others, she didn't want to keep me. This time I hadn't gotten rid of her before she could figure out I wasn't worth keeping. I wanted too much. I'd hoped for too damn much.

Voices drifted across the lawn, and I watched as Eva came walking out the front door with Jeremy and his cousin. I could hear their laughter. The three of them walked out to Eva's Jeep, and the cousin opened her door and whispered something in her ear before helping her get inside. Pain sliced through me.

Jeremy climbed in the back, and his cousin sat in the passenger's seat. Eva was going out. She was moving on. I had been a side distraction.

My eyes stung, and I hated the weakness the tears represented. Fuck that. I wouldn't cry. I didn't cry. I also didn't fucking beg. I knew what it felt like to beg someone to want you. I'd been called a worthless piece of shit by my father from the time I was five. Then again by my mother when I was a teenager rebelling because of the life I'd been handed.

I'd decided long ago that if I was worthless, then I didn't have to live by anyone's fucking rules. I'd make my own.

EVA

My phone chimed, alerting me to a text message, and I grabbed it praying it was Cage. He hadn't come back yet, and it was Tuesday. Daddy didn't seem concerned, and I was scared to ask him where Cage was. I couldn't show any interest in Cage. But I needed to know where he was. He'd stopped texting me after Saturday night. He hadn't called. I'd ignored him. I had to. I was so confused.

The text was from Chad. He was driving me nuts. We'd gone out dancing Saturday night after Cage had left. Daddy and Elaine had thought that was a wonderful idea when Jeremy had suggested it. I had been stuck. Elaine's hopeful expression as Chad pulled my chair out for me had been hard to miss. She had invited Chad because she was matchmaking.

Chad wanted to know what I was doing tonight. I wanted to know when he was going back to Louisiana so he would leave me alone. I typed that I wasn't up for doing anything and left it at that.

Watching the barn for Cage to show up was making me anxious and nauseous every minute he didn't come driving up. Had he quit? Surely not. He had his scholarship to deal with. I looked down at my phone and thought about texting him. I'd ignored his attempts at trying to contact me. Would he even respond?

I had to know.

Me: Are you okay? Where are you?

I held my phone in my hands and waited.

The silence in the room was deafening. I could hear my heart beating. With each second that ticked by without a response, my stomach twisted tighter into the coil it had been in since Elaine had told me how disappointed Josh would be in me. I didn't want to disappoint Josh. I didn't want to make a mistake.

Cage had been a way for me to heal. He'd been fun and exciting. Nothing felt bad and wrong when we were together. I knew he would be gone soon. I hadn't kidded myself into believing we had anything long lasting.

After several minutes and no response I dropped my phone onto the bed and lay back on my pillow. Was he going to leave my life just like that? No good-bye, just disappear?

A warm tear trickled down my cheek. For the first time in eighteen months, my tears weren't because of Josh Beasley.

I decided to go get Cage's sheets and wash them on Wednesday morning. I could ask Daddy if he was coming back with the excuse that I needed to know if I should put the sheets back on once I cleaned them.

The barn door was open when I stepped outside. Hope surged in my chest. I wanted to run toward the barn, but I couldn't. Daddy was around here somewhere.

Once I got close, I stopped and took a deep breath before I walked inside. If he was in there, I had to explain things. I wasn't sure yet what I was going to say. Telling Cage that Josh's mother didn't approve of him wasn't exactly a wise idea. Cage didn't seem like the kind of guy who would take with a shrug being told he was less than worthy. If I wanted to get rid of him, that would be a really good way to do it. And I definitely didn't want to get rid of him.

Cage stalked out of the barn with a scowl on his face. He had a straw hat tilted back on his head, and his shirt wasn't yet soaked from sweat. He was gorgeous.

He halted when he saw me, and then his face turned hard and cold before he continued past me and threw the shovel and toolbox into the back of the truck. I tried to speak, but my words got stuck in my throat. I didn't know how to talk to this Cage. The one with the cocky smile and sexy swagger was gone.

He stalked back by me and headed into the barn. I was frozen. What did I say? Would he yell at me if I tried to explain? Did he even care? Had I been written off where he was concerned? Oh, God. Was I now just one of the many he'd tossed away and forgotten?

He came back out of the barn with his hands full of bags of feed and a can of motor oil. His eyes didn't even flicker past me. I really did feel invisible now.

Once he'd thrown the things in his truck, he headed for the driver's-side door and jerked it open. He was going to drive off. I had to say something.

"Cage?" I croaked out.

The only reason I knew he heard me was that his shoulders tensed, but he didn't look back and respond.

"Cage, please," I begged, hoping that would at least get him to look at me.

His grip on the door was so tight his knuckles were white.

"Don't," he replied in a flat, emotionless voice before sliding inside and slamming the door behind him.

He pulled out and headed south without once making eye contact with me. My chest felt like it was going to burst. I wanted to cry. I wanted to scream. I wanted to run after him and demand he talk to me.

This was what it felt like to care about someone who didn't feel the same.

I'd only known how it felt to love someone who loved me just as fiercely. I'd never known rejection. I'd never wanted someone who didn't want me. The longing didn't go away with rejection.

Numbly, I went inside the barn and headed back to his room. I would still wash his sheets and towels. He needed clean things.

I opened the door to his room. The mattress was bare, and a set of clean sheets was stacked on top. Beside them sat a pile of folded clean towels and washcloths. He'd taken his things to Low. She'd washed them for him.

The sorrow only grew. She'd never have to feel the ache from Cage's rejection. He loved her. He always would. Just like Josh had loved me without question. It had been unconditional. I hated Willow because she had something I never would: Cage York's unconditional love. Did anyone else have that? I knew they didn't. He never spoke of family. Low was his family. She was all that mattered to him. What must that feel like? I picked up his towels and put them on the small shelf beside the shower. Then I went about making up his bed for him. I hadn't been able to clean his sheets for him, but at least I could do something. I wanted to do something for him. Even if he no longer wanted me.

Chapter Twenty

CAGE

She'd made my bed. Dammit. Why was she doing this? For three very long days I'd worked hard to wash my head of her and flush her out of my system. A lot of whiskey and women. It hadn't worked. The only way I'd been able to perform was to close my eyes and pretend it was Eva. Calling out her name hadn't gone over well with the girls who had been sober enough to realize I wasn't mentally with them.

The corner of my quilt was pulled back for me, and a plate of food sat on the table beside it covered in foil to keep it warm. I just had to make it until Saturday night. Then I'd be gone again for three full days. Coach had decided I needed to start working out with the team Sunday through Tuesday. I was just supposed to work here Wednesday through Saturday now. Wilson had given Coach Mack a good report, and I was being rewarded for good behavior.

When Eva had pleaded with me earlier, I'd almost cracked. The only thing that kept me from turning back to look at her had been the image of her with the other guy. She'd let him touch her and help her into the Jeep. He hadn't been snubbed. He was good enough. I couldn't do this with her. Being someone's dirty little secret hadn't bothered me until now. I didn't want to be Eva's secret. Things had been different with her. I'd felt something. It had been real. It had been more. So much more.

I took the foil off the plate, and the smell from the meat loaf and corn hit me. I was ravenous. The image of Eva fixing my plate and carefully wrapping it and bringing it out here to me tugged at my chest. Damned if this wasn't going to be hard. Luckily, I'd learned at an early age that self-preservation was the only way to survive with your soul intact.

Or maybe I'd lost my soul already. I doubted God let someone like me keep any gift from him. It was highly likely I'd been born without one.

The lake water was getting warmer with each smoldering-hot day. It was still cooler than the hundred-degree heat that had gotten so thick it made it hard to take deep breaths. I ducked my head under the surface and soaked my hair, slicking it back off my face.

The sound of a car door slamming caught my attention as I surfaced. I spun around in the water to see Eva walking toward me. Shit. What was she doing now? I'd done everything I could think of to make her leave me the hell alone. Her long brown hair was flying free down her back, and her flat, tanned stomach was bare. The little red halter top she was wearing with them damn cutoff shorts sent my blood pumping.

I should've turned my head away and ignore her, but she was so damn beautiful it was hard. I hadn't allowed myself to stare at her in over a week. She stopped at the bank and started pulling her halter top off. What the fuck? A red lacy bra was covering up her tits, and although I should've been relieved, it wasn't any better than seeing them bare. It was fucking sexy as hell. When her hands went to the snap on her shorts, I opened my mouth to stop her, but she began shimmying out of them. A pair of matching red lace panties with very little coverage caused me to choke on my tongue.

"You are going to talk to me," she demanded, stepping into the water. I wanted to argue with her, but she was walking into the water with red fucking undies on. I couldn't form words.

"Where were you?" she asked as she closed the space between us.

I couldn't forget. I couldn't break. She had the power to break me. No one had ever been given that power, ever. Eva could do it. If I let her in any further, she could completely destroy me. I was weak where she was concerned. I couldn't be weak. She'd rejected me already. Why was she so damned determined to talk to me now? I didn't get rejected. I was the one who rejected. I didn't give someone a chance to decide I wasn't good enough.

"I don't reckon that's your fucking business, now is it, sweetheart?" I drawled in a bored tone.

She stiffened and stopped her approach. Good. If she got too close, I was going to grab her and forget all about how she didn't think I was good enough for her. She was ashamed of me. I held on to that thought as her plump tits played peekaboo with the water. Teasing me.

"Why are you being this way?" she asked. The hurt in her voice put a crack in my wall. I had to get away from her before I made a mistake.

"I'm just being me."

She frowned. "This isn't you. You're not cold and mean."

I clenched my hands into fists under the water to keep from reaching out and pulling her sweet little body up against mine and getting one more taste of her, one more memory to keep with me when I left. She'd rejected me. She would only do it again.

"What ya want, baby? You want me to take care of that hot body you're out here advertising? 'Cause I don't mind making it feel good. You can come all over my fingers, or are you ready for me to bury myself inside you now? You want to know what it's like to fuck a bad boy? It's pretty damn good, or so I've been told. I always have 'em coming back for more."

"Cage, don't do this," she choked out.

"Don't do what? Tell you the truth about me? You had me figured out all along. It's why you want to keep me your dirty little secret. I'm used to that, Eva. I've been lots of women's wild thrill."

"Stop it. That isn't who you are."

I took a step toward her, and my heart hammered against my chest painfully. The tears that filled her eyes were all I could handle. I hated myself as the ugly shit poured out of my mouth. "Yeah, baby, it is. But don't you worry. I'll be fine. I got rejected by you, and more came running. Several hot little sorority girls made me feel all better this weekend."

Before I could get the hell away from her, she spun around and hurried to shore. I started to walk out of the water when the pain in my chest became unbearable. I bent over and put my hands on my knees. FUUUUCK. This hurt.

The Jeep roared to life, and I listened as she drove away. She had run again, but this time I'd sent her running.

I stood up, threw my head back, and yelled, "MOTHER-FUCKER!" as the sun beat down on me. Mocking me. Mocking my life.

EVA

Josh was gone. Jeremy was gone. And now that it was Saturday night, Cage was gone. I had no one. I couldn't stand this. I needed to make the pain go away. I'd been so hurt that staying away from Cage the rest of the week had been the only way I could deal with it. Even then, all I could manage to do was cry. He'd been with other women. I wanted to believe he was lying just to hurt me, but I knew he wasn't. I had seen the sincerity in his eyes.

The idea of someone else touching him and feeling his hands all over her body made me nauseous. I couldn't stand it. I needed to forget. I needed to wash that image in my head away. The pain was only getting worse. He thought I'd rejected him, and in a way, I had. He was right. I deserved this. But it hurt so incredibly bad.

I pulled my Jeep into Nelly's. It was the only honky-tonk in town. It was also the only place a twenty-year-old could get a drink. I needed to feel numb. Alcohol was the only thing I could come up with that would work.

Nelly wasn't above slipping you a drink if you had the money. Because of this, she managed to run a very success-ful business. Out here in the country no one thought to come check her out. She got away with a lot of things because she was off the radar.

I had pulled out the blue jean miniskirt that Josh had loved so much and put it on as a source of comfort. I completed my honky-tonking outfit with cowboy boots and a shiny black halter top. I was going to dance with attractive men and drink enough tequila to make the pain go away. Cage may have thrown me aside once he'd gotten tired of me, but I wasn't undesirable. Many guys would be thrilled to have my attention.

I jerked the door open. As I stepped into the smoky bar, I searched for Becca Lynn. She'd texted me and told me to come meet her here if I was up for some fun. I noticed her dancing with a guy in a black Stetson and a pair of tight jeans. Becca Lynn was rubbing every part of her body against his as the live band played an old country song that reminded me of Daddy's Hank Williams Jr. albums.

Nelly was at the bar, and I headed over to order my first shot of the night.

"Didn't 'spect to see you back here after Jeremy came to peel you off the floor the last time you stopped in." Nelly's concerned frown bothered me. Did everyone in town stick their noses in my business?

"I need a drink, Nelly," I told her as I sat down on the empty stool in front of her.

She sighed. "All righty, girl, reckon you're a woman now." She grabbed a shot glass and poured Jose Cuervo Silver into the glass, then slid it over to me.

"You wanting lime and salt with that?"

"No. This is fine," I replied, and slung it back. The heat

burned all the way down my throat. I put the glass back down and pushed it back to her.

"Easy now, sugar," she chided, and filled the glass again before sliding it back to me.

"I just need two to get me loosened up."

I took the glass and downed it quickly. The burn was less intense, but it was still there.

"This 'cause Jeremy left for school?" Nelly asked, leaning her elbows on the bar, studying me. Her long black hair was peppered with gray and pulled back into a ponytail. Hard living hadn't been good to her, and although she was probably in her mid-forties, she looked older. Her skin was weathered and hard-looking.

"No. This time it isn't because of a Beasley boy," I informed her, sliding my glass to her. "Just one more," I told her.

"Who am I gonna call, with Jeremy gone, if you end up trashed?"

"I won't get drunk, I promise. I just need a buzz, Nelly."

Her wrinkled lips puckered into a frown, and she poured me one more shot.

I didn't wait for her to give it to me. I reached over, picked it up, and downed it. The numbness started to set in, and Cage York seemed less important. Perfect. I smiled at Nelly and would have kissed her sagging cheek if I could've reached her. She'd given me my first relief from the pain since Cage had discarded me.

Standing up, I had to stop a second to steady myself when

the room shifted a little. Once I had my balance, I walked out to the dance floor. I'd dance by myself. I didn't need a man.

"Eva Brooks, I do believe you have been drinking," a familiar voice drawled, and I lifted my gaze from the floor where I'd been focused on not falling over and met the smiling brown eyes of Mark Ganner. Mark had played wide receiver in high school. Josh had often said that Mark was his go-to guy. He could catch a ball no matter how bad the throw.

"Mark." I smiled, glad to see someone from my past.

"You look real good, Eva."

I reached out, grabbed his arm, and leaned on him some. My legs were still a little numb. "Thank you," I replied.

"You wanna dance?" Mark asked.

"YES!"

Mark laughed and pulled me into his arms. I was thankful for some support.

"What have you been up to?" he asked as we moved together to the music.

"Nothing. Trying to figure out what happens next."

Mark nodded. "Yeah."

The song changed, and I had more control over my body as the tequila eased through me. Throwing back my head, I laughed, and I began moving my hips seductively against Mark. The interest in his eyes felt empty. Then again, I was empty. Might as well take what I could get.

"EVA!" Becca Lynn squealed as the cowboy twirled her around, and she sidled up next to Mark and me.

"Look at you, already buzzing and dancing with Mark. I'm so proud I could just bust," Becca cheered. "You be good to her, Mark."

"She's in good hands," Mark assured Becca. She giggled, then threw him a wink before dancing off.

"You two still keeping in touch, then?" Mark asked.

"Yeah, Becca Lynn still comes around. She's about the only friend other than Jeremy who is brave enough to visit me."

Mark frowned, and I could see the pity in his eyes. I hated the pity. Cage never looked at me with the damn pity in his eyes.

"I need another shot. Would you get it for me? Nelly is being stingy tonight with me."

Mark's pity vanished, and he gave me an excited grin. "Yeah, sure. I'll be right back."

"Could you make that two?" I asked as he started toward the bar.

"Absolutely."

Chapter Twenty-One

CAGE

"Get your sorry ass up, and go crook your damn finger and get us a couple hotties. I want a redhead tonight with really big tits. So damn big that they're fake," Preston yelled over the loud music.

"I'm just here to drink," I replied. I'd already told him that once. I just couldn't pretend with cheap sex. It didn't help. It just made me more of a bastard than I already was.

"Come on, man. I can wrangle up some ladies, but you always get the damn cream of the crop. Especially with titties. The girls with big titties flock to you. Please go get me some big round plump tits I can bury myself in tonight."

I liked Preston, but he was getting on my nerves. I didn't want to get him any damn tits. Did he even realize how fucking shallow he sounded?

"I said I wasn't here for that."

Preston set his beer down on the table and took the empty stool beside me. "Please don't tell me this is over the girl you brought in here a few weeks back. I thought you were over that. I can't go through this shit with you, too. First Marcus, now you. Hell, what happened to a variety of pussy? Why would anyone want to give that up?"

My phone vibrated in my pocket before I had to respond to him. I pulled it out and an unfamiliar number flashed on my screen. I answered and covered my other ear so I could hear. "Hello?"

"Cage. Hey, man, this is Jeremy. Where are you?"

What the hell was Jeremy calling me for?

"In Sea Breeze. Why?"

"I need a big-ass favor. It's Eva."

I stood up and started walking for the door in long strides. "What about Eva?"

"I'm in Louisiana, and she's gone and gotten trashed again. I just got a call from Nelly. She said Eva was dancing on the damn bar."

"Fuuuck," I growled, and broke into a run. Digging in my pocket, I found my keys and jammed them into the lock as I reached my Mustang. I wasn't supposed to be driving, but fuck that. I had to get to her. What if someone touched her? My chest pounded frantically in my chest.

"Nelly is watching her, but she said that someone needed to come get her, and she hated to call Wilson. He'd be furious. Besides that, he's gone to the hunting camp to fish."

"Call Nelly and tell her to get Eva off the bar and make sure no one lays a finger on her, or she's gonna have one helluva bar fight on her hands when I get there," I growled.

Jeremy was quiet a second, then finally said, "Okay. I will. Can I ask you something?"

No. "What?"

"Is she just another girl to you? Or is she different?"

I gripped the steering wheel tightly, trying to control the range of emotions rolling through me.

"Eva's always been different," I said through clenched teeth.

"Good." He sighed. "I'll call Nelly."

I slung the phone down onto the passenger seat. This was my fault. If someone touched her, it would be my fault. It would also be my fault when the stupid fucker got his face pummeled.

I pulled into the parking lot of Nelly's and had the door open before I came to a complete stop. I'd managed to make an hour's drive in only thirty minutes. It was a miracle I wasn't behind bars.

The heavy wooden door swung open, and Becca Lynn came tumbling out in a pair of stilettos and hanging on the arm of a wannabe cowboy.

Her glassy eyes met mine, and she gave me a drunken smirk. "Cage York, whatya doin' here?"

"Where's Eva?"

Becca Lynn laughed and then shrugged. "Last I saw her, she was dancin' on the bar."

I stalked past Becca Lynn and went inside. Scanning the room, I searched for Eva.

"You here for Eva?" the bartender called out.

"Yeah," I replied, walking over to her. "Where is she?"

The lady threw a towel over her shoulder and stepped out from behind the bar. "Come with me."

I followed her as she unlocked a door to the left of the bar and stepped into a dark hallway.

"I put her back here. I ain't real crazy about bar fights in here. Jeremy told me the cavalry was coming, and if Eva was dancing on a table you'd tear the place up. So I put her in my office."

The lady opened a door at the end of the hall and stood back. "There ya go. I gotta get back out front. Take your time," she said, and turned to walk back down the hall.

I stepped into the room. One single lamp illuminated the room. Eva lay curled up on the faded sofa in the corner. Her eyes were closed, and she looked so peaceful. God, I'd missed her. I'd held her once when she'd slept like this.

I closed the door behind me and walked over to her. I bent

down in front of her and brushed the curls out of her face. Her eyelashes fluttered against her cheek. I ran my thumb over the soft skin underneath her ear. I'd worried that letting her get too close would break me. Unfortunately, I'd worried about that a little too late. Because I was broken. The Cage I was before Eva no longer existed. As much as I didn't want to admit it, I'd fallen in love with her. I'd allowed someone in, and she hadn't wanted me. I hadn't been good enough. I never was.

Seeing her sweet, perfect, innocent face only drove the nail in farther. I wasn't good enough for her. She deserved another Josh in her life. She deserved a guy who hadn't lived a life so fucked up he could never be good enough. I'd walked too close to heaven and gotten a glimpse. The hell I'd lived before her no longer appealed to me.

I stood up and scooped Eva up into my arms. She cuddled against me. "Cage?" she whispered groggily against my chest.

"Yeah, I'm here, baby. Go back to sleep. I'll get you home."

EVA

I opened my eyes and stared at the ceiling. I was at home. In my bed. But I didn't remember going to bed. It was still dark outside. The clock said that is was four in the morning. A glass of water and a bottle of aspirin sat on the bedside table with a small note.

You may need to take another aspirin when you wake up. Drink the water too. ALL of it.

Cage. I could smell him on my shirt. Jumping up, I ran to the window and looked down at the barn. Was he in there?

I started to run for the stairs, and I caught a whiff of the cigarette smell on my clothes. I stripped down and quickly got a shower. I had to wash off the stench of the bar.

After I was clean and dressed, I ran down to the barn. I didn't knock on his door. Instead I opened it slowly. The moonlight streaming in the window fell over Cage's sleeping form. My heart soared. He'd come to get me. He'd brought me home.

Cage's eyes opened, and he stared at me. I knew I needed to say something, but just seeing him here and knowing he'd come back for me clogged my throat with emotion.

"What're you doing, Eva?" His voice didn't sound angry. It sounded defeated.

"I woke up and I was at home. Then I saw your note and I came to see if you were here," I managed to say. I didn't want him to make me leave.

"I'm here. Now go back to bed," he replied.

"Cage, please talk to me. I miss you." I hadn't meant to sound so pathetic, but I couldn't help it. He'd come for me. I needed to know why. He had to feel something for me. I didn't want to be just another girl he'd enjoyed and thrown to the side.

Being with him had meant something to me. He meant something to me.

Cage let out a weary sigh and sat up. The covers fell away, and his bare chest made me almost forget what I wanted to say.

"You can't say shit like that, Eva. It isn't fair."

"How is it not fair to tell you how I feel? It isn't fair that you just dropped me as soon as you got bored. You just went off and screwed some slut with no problem."

Cage's head snapped up. The angry scowl on his face startled me. "What? I didn't drop you because I got bored. You. Rejected. Me! And fuck that, Eva. *All* I saw while I was with them was you. I closed my fucking eyes and pictured you. Just—you."

He'd been thinking about me. Was I mentally screwed up because hearing him say that made it better? I hated that he had been with other girls, but just knowing that it was hard on him and he'd thought of me eased the pain some. I'd started this. My stupid need to please Josh's mom. He'd never have done it had I not brushed him off. All this heartache just because Josh's mother had made me feel guilty.

"I was confused," I admitted.

Cage let out a hard laugh. "Yeah, well, I wasn't."

I took a step toward him, and he shook his head. "Don't come closer."

"Please listen to me. Let me explain."

He ran a hand through his dark hair, and I could see the

internal battle in his expression. I needed to talk while I had him weak.

"I made a mistake. I listened to someone else who knew nothing about you. I let my fears get the best of me, and I made a very, very bad mistake."

Cage dropped his hand back to his lap, and his sad eyes met mine. "But you listened. Something Josh's mother said made sense to you. As much as I hate to admit it, she was probably right. You were right to back away."

He'd already figured out who had talked to me, and he'd called her Josh's mom, not Jeremy's. He was making this about Josh.

"No, Cage. No, I wasn't."

"Yeah, Eva, you were. I'm not the good guy. I'm not the guy you could ever tell your daddy about. You would be embarrassed to let people in this small town know you'd gone from the great and mighty Josh Beasley to the loser Cage York. You deserve a Josh Beasley."

My heart broke as I watched the self-loathing on Cage's face. I hated myself for putting it there. He wasn't Josh. He was nothing like Josh. He was more.

"Cage, please don't," I begged, closing the distance between us.

He backed away, and I grabbed his face with my hands and covered his lips with mine. He didn't respond at first. When

I straddled his lap and crawled on top of him, he caved. His hands slid up the backs of my legs as he slipped his tongue in my mouth and began kissing me back.

The groan that tore from his chest made me a little crazy. I wanted this so badly. I needed to feel close to him again. I reached for the bottom of my shirt and pulled it off, ignoring Cage's protest. I grabbed his face again, pressing my bare chest against his. The cold barbell tickled my nipple and I shivered.

I tasted him the way he always tasted me. Kissing each corner of his mouth, I nipped at his bottom lip and pulled his tongue into my mouth, sucking it hard. When his hands cupped my breasts, I cried out and pressed down on him. His erection put pressure on my swollen heat. Tonight that wasn't enough. I needed to be closer. I'd almost lost him. I needed more.

I pushed him until he fell back on the mattress underneath me. Seeing him staring up at me with those eyes that reflected what I was feeling sent any doubt from my mind. I stood up and started taking off my shorts.

"Eva, don't . . . ah, fuck," Cage groaned as I stepped out of my panties and crawled back on top of him. I pulled the covers down so I could take his boxers off, and his erection sprang free instead. Cage slept naked. Reaching down, I took him in my hands and slid them down his silky, warm texture.

Cage let out a low moan. "Ahhhh, Eva, you don't want to do this," he said in a hoarse, desperate plea.

Yes, I did. I wanted to do this more than I wanted to breathe. "Put a condom on, Cage."

I watched as Cage leaned over and grabbed a condom from the pocket of his discarded jeans. He ripped open the package with his teeth then slowly rolled it down over himself.

I slid my hands up his chest and lowered my body over his. Keeping my legs on each side of his hips, I closed my eyes in pure pleasure as his erection jerked against my wet opening.

I'd never done this, but I'd read enough to know it would be difficult to do this my first time with me on top. I needed him to take over. I slid over him several times, causing him to curse and grab the sheet under him in a death grip.

"Cage, I want you inside me. I want you to make love to me," I whispered against his ear, and he trembled underneath me. It was a powerful feeling, and I loved it.

Cage moaned and grabbed my waist. He pulled my chest closer to his mouth. When my nipple dangled in front of him, he reached up and covered it with his mouth. Crying out, I pressed his head closer to me. I wanted more.

He bit down gently on my nipple, and I felt a zing shoot through my body.

"Yes, please," I begged. He let it pop out of his mouth before moving to the next breast and doing the same thing to it. I began rocking back and forth. The more he sucked, the better it got.

Cage shifted his hips, and I froze when the head of his

erection entered me. Closing my eyes, I wanted to warn him, but it felt so good I couldn't find words.

"Fuck, baby, you're so damn tight," he groaned as his hands grabbed my hips and held me still. I pressed down, and the pain from the stretching was exciting.

"Stop. Don't. I'll hurt you. Please. Just give me a minute. I need to do this easy." His breathing was labored and his words choppy.

I let him ease me down lower, and I cried out as the pain intensified. He stilled.

"Eva?" he asked in a pained voice. Was I hurting him, too? Was I too tight?

"Yeah?" God, please don't let him stop.

"You're a virgin."

I swallowed nervously. "Yeah."

"Oh, hell," he groaned, and began sliding back out of me.

"No, don't, please," I begged as he lifted me off him.

He flipped me on my back and stared down at me. "I want this. So help me God, I don't deserve this but I want it so fucking bad. Are. You. Sure?" His face was so torn. I reached up and cupped his face, rubbing my thumb across his cheekbone.

"Yes. Please, Cage. This is what I want," I replied.

He closed his eyes and let out a jagged breath. "Okay." He settled between my legs, holding himself over me. "I've never been with a virgin, Eva. I'm going to try real hard not to hurt you."

"Will it hurt you?" I asked, thinking about his pained expression when he'd said I was tight.

He smiled. "It's going to be the closest to heaven I'll ever get, baby."

Oh. My.

I watched his face as he eased inside me. As I stretched to fit him, the pain didn't bother me. Seeing the pleasure on Cage's face as he sank deeper inside me made me want to buck against him. I loved knowing I could make him feel this good.

He came to a stop and his eyes bored into me. "This is the part that will hurt. I'm gonna do it quick, and then I'll be still until you get used to it."

"Okay."

Cage closed his eyes tightly and pressed hard into me, and a sharp pain inside took my breath away. He buried his face in my neck and began raining kisses on all my soft spots while whispering how good I felt. "I'm in, and you're so warm and tight. It's like a damn glove, baby."

Hearing him tell me how it felt for him made my pleasure come back in full force. I wanted him to move. Lifting my hips, he rocked deeper into me.

"Oh God, Eva," he groaned as he slid slowly out, then back inside.

I lifted my legs up to cup his hips, and he let out an approving groan of pleasure.

"That's perfect. You're perfect," he panted.

I didn't want this to end.

His breathing became more ragged and his arms flexed with each thrust.

"Fuck, baby, you're so damn tight," he moaned.

I lifted to meet each thrust, needing something. I needed more. I couldn't get enough.

Cage growled and pulled out of me.

"No, don't," I cried as he spread my legs and buried his face between them. The first lick of his tongue against me sent me soaring. I heard my scream of pleasure and Cage's name rip from my chest as I bucked wildly against his face. He let out a loud moan as he continued.

He slowed down and finally lifted his head. As incredible as that had been, I'd been enjoying having him inside me.

"Why did you stop?"

He wiped his mouth with the back of his hand and crawled back up beside me. "The condom broke. That's never happened before. But I felt it and I had to get out of you before I exploded."

"So you didn't . . ." I trailed off, hating that once again he hadn't gotten off.

He chuckled. "Oh, no, I did. A fucking load."

Frowning, I turned to look up at him.

"I'm gonna need to change the sheets," he explained.

"Oh," I replied. I wanted to do it again, and I wanted him to get off inside me. "Do you have another condom?" I asked, shifting so I could touch his pierced nipple.

"I always have condoms," he replied.

Smiling up at him, I kissed his barbell. "How long until you can do it again?"

He raised both eyebrows in surprise. "It ain't about me. I can do it right now, but you're going to be sore"—he ran his thumb over my bottom lip—"because you were so incredibly fucking tight. I swear, Eva, nothing has ever compared to that."

"I'm not sore," I assured him, shifting my hips so I could straddle him.

"Yeah, you are. Just wait, in the morning you'll feel it."

Pouting, I sat back and crossed my arms under my breasts. His eyes zeroed in on them, and I had a hard time not smiling. "When will we get to do it again?"

Cage leaned up on his elbows, and his eyes locked with mine. "Any damn time you want to. I'm all yours." He smirked. "If you keep pouting, I'm gonna decide your being sore can be dealt with in other ways."

Curious, I leaned over him. "What does that mean?"

He pressed a kiss to the top of one of my breasts. "It means I will just kiss it and make it better."

Chapter Twenty-Two

CAGE

Eva woke me up an hour before dawn, kissing my chest and sliding her hand up and down my very awake cock.

"Mmmm," I moaned, reaching down to pull her closer so I could press her wonderfully swollen lips to mine. "This is the way to wake up," I whispered before slipping my tongue into her eager mouth.

Eva threw her leg over my hips and straddled me.

"What ya doin', baby?" I asked as she leaned up until the head of my dick was penetrating her. "Whoa! Hold up." I reached for the extra condom I'd left on the bedside table last night just in case. "We need to use this."

"Can I do it?" she asked with a wicked grin on her face.

"Oh yeah," I replied, handing the small packet to her.

She ripped it open with her teeth, which was sexy as hell. Then she rolled it down slowly, causing my cock to jerk anxiously under her touch. Once she had it firmly in place, she sat up and sank down on it in one thrust. We both cried out and bucked in unison.

I watched in wonder as Eva slowly opened her eyes and gazed down at me with pure pleasure glittering in her eyes. I'd never get tired of this. Of her. I'd never get enough. I gripped her waist and guided her as she rode me, driving us both closer and closer to the edge.

Just before I lost myself inside her, my mouth opened, and I couldn't hold back the words hammering in my head with each beat of my heart.

"I love you."

When I stepped out of the shower, my sheets were gone. If I hadn't shot my load on them, I'd have wanted to keep them. They smelled like sex and Eva. I grabbed a towel and dried my hair. Then I wrapped the towel around my waist. I'd been worried about making Eva sore, but damned if she hadn't made me sore.

After last night, Eva owned me. I pushed away the fear that came with that knowledge. Before, I thought she'd broken me, but now she had the power to absolutely destroy me. Sex had always been a release for me. Nothing more than a pleasurable pastime. What we'd done had been so much more than sex.

A sharp knock on the barn door snapped me out of my happy thoughts.

"Yeah?" I called out.

The door swung open, and Wilson came storming inside with murder on his face. It didn't take much for me to figure out I was the one he was ready to kill. Somehow—he knew.

He pointed his finger in my face. "You touched something you had no business touching, boy. She ain't one of your little sluts. She's a good girl who has had one helluva hard time. I ought to put a bullet through your head and bury you in the yard," he ranted, and shook his finger at me. "But I ain't. I've called Mack. I've told him that you worked hard here this summer and that you should be let off for your DUI and allowed back on the team. I didn't tell him you've been banging my little girl. It took all my willpower not to grab my shotgun and come blow your fucking balls off when I drove up to see Eva walking out of here at sunrise with her arms full of YOUR SHEETS!"

Had Eva seen him? Was she okay? Why hadn't she called or texted me to warn me?

"You will pack your bags and walk out to that little car of yours and drive away. You won't tell her bye. You won't even look her way. If you so much as blink in her direction, I will make sure you lose everything. I know all about your situation. You want a future? Then you can't lose your education. If you want to keep it, then you'll walk. Don't kid yourself, boy. If you think you can choose my daughter instead, you'll never have her. I'll go get that gun and I'll put an end to it that way. You hear me?"

He wanted me to walk away from her? How the fuck was I supposed to walk away from her? I couldn't leave her.

"I won't leave her."

"The hell you won't. You won't ever have her. I can pick up the phone right now and take away your world."

Baseball was the only way that I would get a college education. I wouldn't have another chance. I'd be working in a bar somewhere making minimum wage and tips for the rest of my life. Eva deserved more than that. She deserved a man who could take care of her. But fuck if I was just going to leave her. I couldn't do that. I might not be good enough for her, but I was gonna damn well try my hardest to become worthy.

"I can't hurt her, and I will not leave her."

"You already did hurt her, boy. You already did. She was unstable, and you took advantage of that. Eva won't ever marry someone like you. She loved Josh Beasley. She adored him. She will never be happy until she finds another Josh. We both know you ain't ever gonna meet those standards. You are just a way for Eva to act out. You don't mean anything to her, boy. Now pack up and go before I change my mind."

Wilson slammed the door on his way out.

I sank down on the bed and dropped my head into my hands. *Marry?* Fuck, what did he mean by "marry"? I couldn't get married. Eva would never think of me that way. I wasn't the kind of guy a girl like her married. He was right. I was Eva's side thrill. She'd never said she loved me. She'd never said anything about forever. I would never measure up to Josh, and Eva wanted another Josh. She deserved another Josh. When Eva decided to get married, she'd go looking for someone without a fucked-up past and a criminal record.

Last night I'd made love to a woman for the first and last time. It had been amazing, and I had a memory that would shape the rest of my life. Eva got her taste of the wild side. She'd move on soon enough. It wasn't as though I was breaking her heart. But damn if I wasn't ripping mine out of my chest.

With my duffel bag packed up, I headed out to my car. I didn't look anywhere but straight ahead. I wouldn't be able to leave if I saw her. She might not love me, but I loved her so damn much it wouldn't matter. The closer I got to my car without her calling out my name, the more I felt something inside me die.

Opening the car door, I threw my duffel inside. I pulled out of the drive for the last time. Leaving my heart behind.

EVA

Where was he? After I'd gotten a shower, I'd taken extra-special care fixing my makeup and picking out an outfit that would make Cage crazy. Then I'd gone downstairs to fix him breakfast.

His car was gone. I walked outside and looked around for it. My heart started racing as fear settled in. Had something happened? Was he okay? Had he gotten in trouble for driving last night? I ran down to the barn and into his bedroom. It was empty. No sign that Cage had ever been there.

I turned around and found my daddy standing at the door.

"What're you doing, Eva?"

I didn't care anymore. Daddy could get over it. I was twenty years old. "I'm looking for Cage," I replied, daring him to ask me why.

"He left."

My heart stopped. "What do you mean?" Had he needed to take his car back? Did he have practice?

"Mack wanted him back. Said he'd done his sentence and he could come on back home. He ran outta here like he couldn't wait to get away."

No. No. Cage wouldn't just run off. He wouldn't go without telling me when he'd see me again. My phone. Had he called my phone? I pushed past Daddy and ran for the house. I had to get my phone. I'd left it to charge in my room. Maybe it had been on silent and I'd missed his call. That had to be it, because Cage would not leave me. Not after last night. He wouldn't. The last time, when the condom hadn't broken and he'd come while still inside me, he'd said he loved me.

He wouldn't leave me.

There were no calls on my phone. No text messages. Nothing. Cage had left without a word.

Why? What had I done wrong? Had it all been just sex for him? Were all those sweet words something he told every girl when he had sex? God, no. I dropped my phone on the floor and let the pain assail me. I'd given my heart away to someone who didn't want it. Even knowing that, I didn't regret it. I just wanted him to want me. I just wanted him to love me, too.

I took my guitar and headed for the barn. It was my daily routine. Daddy was bothered by it, but I told him to leave me alone and let me handle this the way I wanted to. I wasn't innocent and full of dreams and fantasies anymore. All of that had died with Josh. I understood that pain was real and sometimes things didn't last. Sometimes you just had to enjoy it while it lasted and cherish it when it was gone.

I opened the door to Cage's room, then sat down on the bed and set my guitar in my lap. I'd hid from my music when I'd lost Josh. I needed it now. There was so much I needed to express, and this was the only way I knew how. I opened the new notebook I'd bought, and the words I'd been working on covered the first page. I began playing the tune that I'd heard in my head and jotting down notes that worked better.

My time with Cage wasn't something I ever wanted to forget.

I wanted every emotion written down. The way it felt falling in love. Losing yourself to someone. Those were moments that I would always hold close.

Josh had always been in my life. I don't remember actually falling in love with him. I just always loved him. He was secure. He was there for me, and I knew it. We were a part of each other.

Cage was so different. He'd shown me how it felt to want, to need, to surrender, to lose myself. He encouraged me to let go of my insecurities and be myself. Cage was free and wild. He was like a beautiful bird you could never own.

The words flowed out of me, and I ignored the tears that streaked down my face.

Chapter Twenty-Three

CAGE

"You won't come to the party, so I brought the party to you," Preston called out as he walked into my apartment. Four giggling females followed him inside. Shit.

I slammed my beer down on the counter and glared at him from across the bar. "I told you I wasn't interested."

Preston had his arm around a redhead and reached over to grab her tits. "But look at these beauties." He winked at me. "They're naughty little sorority girls. Our favorite kind."

This was sick. I shoved off from the bar and pointed to the door. "Take them somewhere else, Preston. I'm not in the mood."

A blonde sauntered over to me and pressed her massive fake tits against my arm. "Awww, don't be so mean. I can make you feel so much better." When her hand ran over my uninterested cock and squeezed, I snapped.

"Get them the *fuck* out of my apartment. Now."

"Damn, Cage. You're no fun at all anymore."

I didn't wait for him to take them out. I stalked back to my room and slammed the door, then locked it. I'd met girls like those before. They didn't take no for an answer.

"Can I at least use the guest bedroom? I can take care of all four by myself!" Preston called out.

"NO!"

I heard grumbling as they left. Once the door had closed behind them, I lay back on my bed and closed my eyes.

Eva. God, I missed her so much. I went to sleep thinking about her and woke up every morning with the reality that I'd never hold her again.

Did she think I had just left her? Did she think I'd gotten what I'd wanted and left? She'd given me her virginity, and I'd just left. Fuck. How was I going to live the rest of my life knowing she thought I'd just left her? She hadn't called or texted me. Maybe she was relieved. Maybe in the light of day she'd realized she'd made a mistake. I'd told her I loved her. I hadn't been able to hold it in. Other than Low, I'd never told anyone I loved them.

I reached for my phone. Wilson had told me not to contact her, but I had to make sure she was okay.

Me: I'm sorry. I had to leave. I just want to
make sure you're okay.

I doubted she'd reply. But I had to try.

Eva: I'm sorry too.

What did that mean? She was sorry I'd left? She was sorry her
dad had given me no choice? She was sorry she'd had sex with me?

Me: What are you sorry for?
Eva: Everything.

I let my phone fall to the bed, and I closed my eyes against
the pain.

"Come out of that room and get your butt in here," Low
called from my living room. I really needed to hide the extra key
in a better spot.

Rolling over in bed, I stood up and dragged myself into the
kitchen.

"What're you doing here, Low?"

Low took in my appearance and shook her head. "You look
awful. You need to get a shower and shave."

"Thanks. If that's all you wanted to tell me, I'm going back
to bed," I grumbled.

"No, you're not. I came over here because we need to talk."

I leaned against the counter and crossed my arms over my chest. "Talk," I replied.

Low pulled herself up to sit on the bar. "Why are you doing this to yourself? Why did you leave if you were just going to waste away in your apartment?"

Sighing, I ran my fingers through my bed head. "I told you, Low, her dad made me."

"When has anyone ever made *you* do anything? Hmmm? Because the Cage I've known all my life does what he damn well pleases, and screw the rules."

"Even if I had stayed, she wouldn't have ever wanted me. She didn't want me for anything more than a summer fling. I was a way of moving on for her."

Low shook her head. "I don't believe that. I met her. I saw the way she looked at you. She isn't the kind of girl who just messes around for fun."

"She rejected me, Low. When it came down to it and she had to choose her family and friends or me, she chose them. Yeah, I forgave that and took her back, but she was extremely persuasive. She rejected me once. She'll do it again. When things get tough, it will never be me she chooses."

"And you know this because she made one bad decision? She was put on the spot and panicked, Cage."

I shoved off from the counter. I didn't want to get angry

with Low. I'd never been mad at her, but she was pushing me. I wasn't going to be able to control my emotions over this.

"I. Love. Her." I said in hard, clipped words.

"Then take your own advice. Take. A. Chance."

Take a chance. I'd told her that about Marcus. She'd been worried he'd leave her one day. Like me, she was scared of rejection. I'd told her to give Marcus a chance.

"I knew Marcus loved you," I replied.

Low took a step toward me. "And I know anyone you let get close to you the way you let Eva won't be able to *not* love you. It would be impossible. You have no idea how special you are. You see the bad. You've always just seen the bad. But I see the good. There is so much that is good and wonderful about you. You let Eva see that. You've never let anyone else see it before, except me. But you let her. I know that she can't help but love what she saw."

Tears were streaming down Low's face when she finished.

I pulled her into a hug.

"Thank you," I whispered as I rested my chin on the top of her head.

"Don't thank me. Just go get her."

EVA

I stepped out of the barn just as Mrs. Elaine drove up. I hadn't been expecting her, but that didn't mean anything. She used to drop by to see me often. With Jeremy gone off to school, she was probably just needing to talk about him.

"Sure is good to see you with that guitar again." She smiled brightly.

I walked up the porch steps toward her and opened the door.

"It's nice to be playing it again. You want to come in?"

"Yes, I wanted to come talk to you for a little bit."

Great. Another heart-to-heart. The last one had caused a lot of heartache. This time I was going to remember I wasn't a kid who needed guidance, but an adult who knew her own mind.

"Of course, come on in."

I set my guitar case on the table and went to the counter to get two glasses of sweet tea. Mrs. Elaine loved sweet iced tea.

"I hear from your daddy that the boy who was helping out is gone," she said from behind me. My stomach knotted up. I didn't want to talk about Cage with her. I couldn't. She didn't understand. No one did.

"Yeah, he is."

"That's good. He just wasn't the kind of boy you needed to be around. There are such good boys out there. Boys who will make good husbands and fine men."

If she wasn't Josh and Jeremy's mother, and if she hadn't been there for me growing up, I'd show her the door. I owed her respect for those things, and biting my tongue was best. I would just nod and then get rid of her.

"You know, Chad has been asking about you a lot. He talks to me when Jeremy comes home. I think he is smitten with you." She grinned as if she had just let me in on a big secret. I was aware Chad liked me. He wasn't being secretive about it. The texts were getting on my nerves. I'd asked Jeremy to tell him to stop.

"He is going to inherit all that land and the construction company from his dad, ya know. He's a great catch."

He was also a momma's boy who whined when he didn't get his way. His chest was also scrawny and thin. Once you'd touched Cage York's chest, there was no settling for less.

"Hmmm," I replied, taking a big gulp of my tea. Please let this conversation end soon.

"I'm having Chad and his parents down Labor Day weekend. Jeremy will be home too. I thought maybe you would like to come over and celebrate with us. It will be the same thing we do every year. Ribs on the grill. My potato salad you love so much, and green bean casserole."

"Um, well, uh, thank you, Mrs. Elaine, but I'm not sure yet what Daddy is planning on doing and—"

"Oh, he is invited too, of course. We haven't had a gathering between our families on a holiday since before Josh passed away. This will be good for all of us."

The sounds of a door slamming and yelling interrupted our conversation. I jumped up and ran out on the porch. Daddy was blocking my view. I couldn't see who he was yelling at, but I knew the car he was standing in front of. It was Cage. What was he doing here?

"Oh my. What is that boy doing here? Should I call the cops?"

"Shhh, no. Don't call anyone," I snapped, and turned my attention back to the driveway.

"I told you not to come back around here, boy," Daddy roared.

"I shouldn't have left. I want to talk to Eva. You never should've made me leave without talking to her," Cage replied.

What?

"I gave you a choice, and you chose your baseball career over her. Ain't no boy good enough for my girl who would choose anything else over her."

Cage slammed his fist down on his car hood. "I didn't choose anything over her. You threatened my life and my education. It was never about baseball. Fuck baseball!"

"Get in that car and leave. Don't come back. I'll call the cops next time, and you'll go to jail. Don't mess with me. I protect what's mine."

Cage's eyes shifted, and our gazes locked. I didn't understand what I'd just heard. I didn't know what had happened between my daddy and Cage. At the moment I didn't care. I was getting to look at him again. He was here, and I could see him. He didn't look like a guy who wanted to throw me aside.

"I love you, Eva Brooks. No matter what you've been told or what you think of me. I love you!"

Everything and everyone melted away. Cage was yelling for everyone to hear that he loved me. Even with my daddy breathing down his neck. I couldn't move. I didn't know what to do. He had left me. Without saying a word. Now he was back, and he said he loved me. What was the truth? Love didn't just run off without an explanation. He'd broken my heart.

Cage turned to open his car door and climbed inside. Numbly, I watched him pull out and drive away.

I let him go. Why had I let him go?

Chapter Twenty-Four

CAGE

Sitting at our table at Live Bay seemed empty. Everything seemed empty. I'd thought going to see Eva and telling her I loved her would do something. Low had gotten me to believe someone like Eva could love me. She was wrong. Eva had chosen her family over me again. She always would.

"Smile. You're depressing as shit," Rock grumbled as he slammed a beer down in front of me.

"Thanks," I replied.

"Never thought I'd see you with a broken heart. Out of all of the guys, I never thought it'd be you. It's like I've walked into the fucking Twilight Zone and can't get out."

I grunted and took a long swallow of my beer.

"Wanna dance, Cage?"

I didn't even try to remember her name. She was one of the mistakes. I had so many. I just shook my head and took another drink.

"Sorry, honey, but he ain't real good company right now," Trisha apologized for me.

"If you change your mind—" she started.

"I won't," I interrupted her.

She got the hint and walked off. I never even looked at her face. They all looked the same anyway. They all weren't Eva.

"You think maybe you could be less scary?" Trisha asked.

"No."

Rock chuckled. "Let it go, babe. He's nursing a broken heart, and you know that boy ain't ever had one before. It's a new experience for him."

"You may want to warn Krit before they take a break. I don't want Cage and him getting into it because Krit can't keep his mouth shut."

I didn't belong here. I didn't want to be here. I laid a couple twenties on the table and stood up. "I'm leaving, anyway. I've had all the fun I can handle for one night."

"I hate for you to be alone. You want me to call Low?"

Low was the last person I wanted to talk to. She didn't understand that it wasn't an easy fix.

"No. I just want to go home and go to bed. I need to be at the gym in the morning."

"Later," Rock added with a nod, and I turned and headed for the door.

I noticed that Jackdown had stopped playing and the crowd had gone silent. That was odd and unheard of. I paused and looked back at the stage to see what I was missing that had quieted the crowd.

"Hello," Eva's voice said over the microphone. What the fuck?

"I don't, uh, I don't normally play in front of people. Actually, I've never really played in front of people other than my family."

I began walking toward the sound of her voice. I pushed through the crowd and kept my eyes focused on the stage until I was close enough to see her. She stood in the spotlight with her hair pulled back in a ponytail and her guitar across her chest. Those blue eyes that had stopped my heart the first time she'd looked at me found me in the crowd. A small smile touched her lips.

"But I have this song that I wrote for this amazing guy who completely changed my life, and I need him to hear it."

She was going to play and sing in front of a bar full of people. I took another step toward her and she began to play.

"I didn't want to see you, but you invaded my world.
Every dark corner you found a way in

Bringing color to the lifeless and lost.
"I didn't want to touch you, but you reached inside me.
Every lost memory you found a way to melt the frost
Until the small, closed world inside opened up into the sea.

"You made me love you by the smile on your face, the
kindness in your eyes, and the heat of your skin.
One kiss makes all that's been hurt fade away.
You made me love you for the man inside. The one no one sees
but me. The man who listens to what my heart has to say.

"I didn't want to love you, but you're impossible not to love.
Every perfect moment I spend in your arms draws me closer
Showing me that life isn't over because its path takes a
sudden turn.

"I didn't see you coming when you arrived.
Nothing prepared me for the gift of a second chance.
I've been loved in life, but all that matters now is that I'm
loved by you.

"You made me love you by the smile on your face, the
kindness in your eyes, and the heat of your skin.
One kiss makes all that's been hurt fade away.
You made me love you for the man inside. The one no one sees

but me. The man who listens to what my heart has to say.

"I'll spend eternity in your arms if you'll trust me when I say

that I love you."

The roar of the crowd dwindled away as I jumped up on the stage and pulled her into my arms.

EVA

Cage picked me up and carried me off the stage while the crowd cheered and shouted all kinds of suggestions at him. He kept walking until he got to a back door. He opened it and pushed me into a room that looked like a dressing room. Red velvet couches and large mirrors lined the walls.

Closing the door behind him, he clicked the lock. Then he spun me around and pressed me up against the door. His mouth covered mine in a hungry growl, and I wrapped my legs around his waist and grabbed on to his thick, corded arms.

His mouth pressed hungrily against mine as he tasted me thoroughly.

Once he had me panting for breath, he broke the kiss and buried his head in the curve of my neck.

"I fucking love you."

I giggled. That was a very Cage response.

"I do. I swear it. I never should have left. I was scared. I was stupid. I will make it up to you for the rest of our lives."

"Do I get to decide the ways you can make it up to me?" I teased, and I could feel his mouth smile against my neck.

"As long as it's naughty," he replied.

I ran my hands through his hair and down his arms as we stood there.

"You played for me," he said, lifting his head so he could look into my eyes.

"I did."

"It was amazing." He pressed a kiss to my jawline. "Will you sing it for me again sometime?"

"Yes," I replied, unable to keep from laughing.

"I like this skirt," he whispered as his hands slid up my thighs and cupped my panty-covered bottom. "I like it a lot." His hands slid into my panties. When his finger slid inside me, I cried out and he covered my mouth with his. I kissed him back with all the need and desire rolling through me. I began grabbing at his shirt as we kissed frantically. Cage let me slide down his body and stand up so I could pull his shirt off.

I slung it onto the floor, and my mouth covered his nipple, causing him to moan. "Fuck, I'm getting the other one done tomorrow," he swore. The idea of it made me a little crazier. Every night in bed I'd been replaying how incredible sex was with Cage. Now I had him here, and he was all mine. I dropped to my knees to begin unfastening his jeans and then jerked them down as he pulled a small foil packet out of his back pocket and ripped it open. He quickly rolled the condom down over his erection. He reached for me and picked me up, pushing me back against the door. He reached under my skirt, ripped my panties off, and threw them aside. My shirt went next, and his mouth covered my nipple as he lifted me up against the door and slid inside me with one swift thrust.

I cried out, and Cage kissed me hard and thrust his tongue into my mouth the same way he was thrusting into me. Pulling back, he stared down at me.

"Fuuuuuck," he groaned, and I lifted my hips to press him in harder. "Easy, baby," he said through clenched teeth.

"Please, Cage, I want it hard." His eyes flashed bright blue. He pumped into me hard, and I cried out, encouraging him. Each moan of pleasure made him a little wilder. I wanted him wild.

"Ohgod, Eva," he groaned, and pumped faster.

"Yes, yes, YES!"

"Oh, fuck, baby," he cried out, and began pounding into me, causing the door behind us to rattle.

"Harder, Cage. Harder," I begged.

"AHHHH!"

Our bodies grew sweaty, and our frenzied need for release took over.

Neither of us cared about the fact that we weren't muffling our sounds. We just needed release.

"SHIT! I think the condom broke again," Cage growled as he tensed underneath me.

"Don't care, don't stop." I panted desperately.

"I've got to," his body trembled under my hands.

"Please, GOD, just don't stop," I cried out.

Cage let out a roar and began pumping into me again, which sent me spiraling off into bliss.

I felt him leave me instantly and his cry of pleasure followed mine.

"I was just paranoid. It didn't break," he said once he was able to catch his breath.

A smile tugged at my lips.

I was taking the bad boy off the market for good.

Chapter Twenty-Five

EVA

"If you don't stop wiggling in my lap, we aren't gonna get this damn piercing," Cage growled in my ear, causing me to giggle.

"Sorry, I'll be good," I promised.

"I never said I wanted you to be good, baby. I like you bad and naughty." He kissed my shoulder and slipped his finger up between my legs. "And wet."

I pushed his hand away and checked the door to make sure the girl who was going to pierce his other nipple wasn't watching us. "If you don't want me to wiggle, then don't talk dirty," I hissed.

Cage smirked. "That ain't dirty, baby. That's just a little sweet talkin'. But if you want me to talk dirty, I will."

"I want your other nipple pierced. Stop trying to distract me."

Cage nipped at my ear. "I know you want this, and it's making me hot thinking about that little pink tongue of yours going at it like it's fucking candy."

"You are like one large piece of candy. Everything about you is lickable. Even those dimples in your lower back."

His grin spread across his face slowly. "I like it when you lick those, too. I bet we can get them to give us a private room if you want to show me exactly what all parts of my body you like to lick."

The door opened and a girl walked in. She had several tattoos, and most of her face was pierced. Her eyes took in Cage. Which just helped prove what I'd said about him being like one large piece of candy. She saw it too.

"Okay, so you want your other nipple pierced," she said, pulling up a chair and getting her supplies ready.

"She wants my other nipple pierced," he replied, winking at me.

The girl shifted her eyes to me. I could see the envy in them, and I didn't blame her.

"Shirt off," the girl instructed.

I reached down and pulled his shirt up. He lifted his arms obediently.

I cut my eyes over to the girl, and she was enjoying the show. It annoyed me some, but I snuggled closer in his lap, and his arm tightened around me as he tucked his hand between my legs.

"You ready?" she asked him.

"You have no idea," he replied in an amused tone. I bit my lip to keep from laughing.

The girl rubbed alcohol on his nipple, causing it to harden. She then reached for a clamp-type thing that pulled his nipple out. Then came the needle. I tensed in Cage's lap, and he chuckled, slipping his hand up the insides of my thighs. He wasn't even worried about it.

When the needle went in, he didn't even react. I squealed a little, but that was the only reaction.

The small silver barbell went in next.

"You're done," the girl announced, and I sighed in relief.

"You need to keep it clean, and no foreign substances on it until it heals." She looked at me, and I wondered if that meant my saliva.

"Got it," Cage replied, standing up and taking my hand.

"You want me to put my shirt back on?" Cage asked.

I considered all the females between here and the car and nodded.

He reached over and picked it up, then pulled it over his head.

"Come on. I'm ready to go see how much you like it." He grinned wickedly.

"Isn't my saliva a foreign substance? And won't it be sore?"

Cage leaned down and whispered in my ear, "Your saliva is fine, and as for sore, that never stopped us before."

CAGE

Eva fidgeted nervously with her hands on the ride back from her house to get all her things to my apartment. She'd handled her dad like a pro and had had no problem packing up all her things. Now it was obvious something was bothering her. I didn't like things to bother her.

"What's with the fidgeting hands?"

Eva stopped instantly and let out a small laugh. "I didn't realize I was doing that."

"Which is what bothers me. Why are you nervous?"

She bit the inside of her cheek, which was another nervous habit of hers, then cut her eyes over to me, "You sure you want me to answer this?"

I had a brief moment of panic, but I reminded myself that she'd just announced to her father that she was in love with me.

"Yeah, I do," I replied cautiously.

She let out a sigh and shrugged. "I'm worried that this is too soon. What if you get tired of having me around all the time? What if I eat your Wheaties or leave my makeup out in the bathroom, or what if I snore?"

Relief washed over me. This I could fix. She wasn't about to bolt on me.

I pulled into the parking spot under our apartment, then cut the engine and turned in my seat to look at her. "I don't eat Wheaties. I hope you leave all your girlie shit lying all over the place so I can see it when you're not there and know you're coming back. And you don't snore. You do this soft purring thing that is so fucking cute I just want to lie awake and listen to you."

Eva leaned across the console and gave me a soft, quick peck. "I love you."

The goofy grin those words always put on my face couldn't be helped. "Then come upstairs and show me how much you love me. I got all kinds of ideas."

Eva reached over and gently pinched my newest piercing. "Can these be involved?" she asked in a husky voice that instantly made me hard.

"Hell yeah, they can."

Getting Eva up to the apartment so I could have my wicked way with her did sound appealing, but that wasn't what I was excited about. I had a surprise waiting on her, and I couldn't wait to get up there and show her. I carried two of her boxes in my arms and set them down beside the door so I could unlock it. I also didn't want anything in my arms obstructing my view of Eva's face when she walked into the apartment.

I turned the knob slowly and pushed it open.

"Ladies first," I said, stepping back to let her go inside.

Eva gave me a small, confused smile and stepped into the room. I followed her inside, never once taking my eyes off her face. The moment she saw the piano sitting in the middle of the living room with a dozen red roses lying on top of it, she froze.

Her jaw dropped, and then she walked slowly toward the piano. I didn't breathe. I couldn't. I needed her to say something. Had I done the wrong thing getting it for her?

Eva ran her fingers over the ivory keys, and then she reached over and picked up the small card I'd left with the roses. It said simply, *I love you.*

When her eyes lifted to meet mine, they were shining with unshed tears. Her fist came up and covered her mouth, and she shook her head. Ah, shit. I'd made her cry. That was not what I'd wanted to do.

"I can't believe you got me a piano." She breathed out as she dropped her fist from in front of her mouth.

"If you don't want it, we don't have to keep it. I just thought that since you said—"

"You're not taking my piano anywhere," Eva interrupted me. A smile broke across her face, and a small laugh fell from her lips. "You got me a piano," she said, shaking her head like she couldn't quite comprehend it.

"You wanted one," I replied.

Eva set the card back down on the piano and walked over to stand in front of me. She placed both her hands on my chest and stared up at my face. "Cage, I am going to want a lot of things, but I don't expect you to supply those things for me. What I want most is *you.* And I got *you.* Somehow, I snagged the famous playboy Cage York, and I don't intend to let him go."

Smirking, I reached down and touched her bottom lip with the pad of my thumb. "So, you mean I didn't have to buy that piano in order to bribe you to stay? Well, hell, baby. If I'd known that, I could have saved myself a whole lotta money."

Eva burst into laughter and slapped my chest. "Here I am trying to be sweet, and you're making fun of me."

"I'm sorry. I didn't know you wanted to be sweet. I got an idea—let's go take a shower and you can let me taste and see just how sweet you are."

"You aren't gonna let me play with my piano first?" she asked, looking back longingly at her gift.

"I don't mind tasting you on the piano. That's good for me too. I bet you'd look awfully sexy spread out on that bench."

Epilogue

"I talked to Jeremy today. He's doing great at LSU, and I think he met a girl. The majority of our conversation was about how smart she was and how funny she was and how pretty her hair was." I laughed softly, letting the autumn breeze carry my voice.

"He was there when I needed him. You would have been proud of how strong he was, when I knew he was breaking apart inside. You always did say he was the tough one."

I smiled, thinking of the time they'd both gotten their wisdom teeth removed and Josh had been in bed for days in pain, while Jeremy had gone on to football practice the very next day.

"The last time I was here, I was a mess. You'd just shattered my world. I couldn't imagine how I would take the next breath without you, much less how I would live a lifetime alone. I didn't understand your letter then. I didn't think you understood the impact of what had happened. How you could tell me that life would go on and I needed to move on. It was unfathomable to me. You were my world, Josh. From the time I was a little girl until I was eighteen. Every memory I have of growing up has you in it."

I reached into my pocket and pulled out a letter I'd stayed up late last night writing. I couldn't sleep because I'd known I was coming back here today. I had so many things to say, and I wanted to say them right.

"I wrote you a letter this time," I explained.

Opening the stiff paper I'd torn from my notebook, I realized there were no tearstains on this letter. My tears were all dried up now. I'd found my peace.

Dear Josh,

Thank you for giving me the most amazing memories. My life growing up was so full because you were in it. Having your love and loving you were always just right. It made sense. You were my home. When I was with you, I knew everything would be okay.

You dried my tears for me when I was sad. You held my hand when we buried my mother. You made me laugh when the world seemed like it was falling apart. You were every special memory a girl could have. That first kiss will forever be embedded in my brain. It was as funny as it was sweet.

Our life together molded me into the woman I've become. I understand what it feels like to be loved and cherished, because I had that with you. I never doubted my worth, because you taught me I was worthy.

When you said that one day I would heal, I didn't believe that was possible. Life couldn't go on without my best friend. There was no room for another guy in my heart. It turns out you were right. You always were. I found him. He is incredible. He is nothing at all like I would have planned. He doesn't fit into a perfect package. He managed to wriggle into my heart and take over before I knew what was happening. I found that happiness you told me would come along. I'm going to go live that life. I'm sure it will be a wilder ride than I ever imagined, and I can't wait to live it. He's my home now. I'll always love you. I'll never forget you. But this is my good-bye. I wasn't ready before to let you go. Now I can move on. Your memory will live on in my heart always.

Love,
Your Eva Blue

Will Preston's dark secrets be too much for Amanda . . .
Find out in this sneak peek of

just for now

PRESTON

The bottom step was rotten. I needed to put fixing that on my priority list. One of the kids was going to run down it and end up with a twisted ankle—or worse, a broken leg—if I ignored it. Stepping over it, I walked the rest of the way up the steps to my mother's trailer.

It had been a week since I'd stopped by and checked on things. Mom's latest boyfriend had been drunk, and I'd ended up taking a swing at him when he'd called my seven-year-old sister, Daisy, a chickenshit for spilling her glass of orange juice. I'd busted his lip. Mom had screamed at me and told me to get out. I figured a week was enough time for her to get over it.

The screen door swung open, and a big gap-toothed smile greeted me.

"Preston's here!" Brent, my eight-year-old brother, called out before wrapping his arms around my legs.

"Hey, bud, what's up?" I asked, unable to return the hug. My arms were full of groceries for the week.

"He brought food," Jimmy, my eleven-year-old brother, announced, and stepped outside and reached for one of the bags I was carrying.

"I got these. There's more in the Jeep. Go get 'em, but watch that bottom step. It's about to go. I gotta fix it."

Jimmy nodded and hurried off toward the Jeep.

"Did you get me dose Fwooty Pebbles I wyke?" Daisy asked as I stepped into the living room. Daisy was developmentally delayed in her speech. I blamed my mother's lack of caring.

"Yep, Daisy May, I got you two boxes," I assured her, and walked across the worn, faded blue carpet to set the bags down on the kitchen counter. The place reeked of cigarette smoke and nasty.

"Momma?" I called out. I knew she was here. The old beat-up Chevelle she drove was in the yard. I wasn't going to let her avoid me. The rent was due. I needed any other bills that may have come in the mail.

"She's sweepin'," Daisy said in a whisper.

I couldn't keep the scowl off my face. She was always sleeping. If she wasn't sleeping, she was off drinking.

"The dickhead left her yesterday. She's been holed up pouting ever since," Jimmy said as he put the other groceries down beside mine.

Good riddance. The man was a mooch. If it wasn't for the kids, I'd never show up at this place. But my mom had full custody because in Alabama as long as you have a roof and you aren't abusing your kids, then you get to keep them. It's some fucked-up shit.

"You bought free gaddons of milk?" Daisy asked in awe as I pulled out all three gallons of milk from a paper bag.

"'Course I did. How are you gonna eat two boxes of Fruity Pebbles if you don't have any milk?" I asked, bending down to look her in the eyes.

"Pweston, I don't think I can dwink all free," she said in another whisper. Dang, she was cute.

I ruffled her brown curls and stood up. "Well, I guess you'll have to share with the boys, then."

Daisy nodded seriously like she agreed that was a good idea.

"You bought pizza rolls! YES! Score," Jimmy cheered as he pulled out the large box of his favorite food and ran to the freezer with it.

Seeing them get excited over food made everything else okay. I'd gone weeks with nothing but white bread and water when I was their age. Momma hadn't cared if I ate or not. If it hadn't been for my best friend, Marcus Hardy, sharing his lunch with me every day at school, I'd have probably died from malnutrition. I wasn't about to let that happen to the kids.

"I thought I told you to get out. You caused enough trouble 'round here. You run off, Randy. He's gone. Can't blame him after you broke his nose for nothin'." Momma was awake.

I put the last of the cans of ravioli in the cabinet before I turned around to acknowledge her. She was wearing a stained robe that was once white. Now it was more of a tan color. Her hair was a matted, tangled mess, and the mascara she'd been wearing a few days ago was smeared under her eyes. This was the only parent I'd ever known. It was a miracle I'd survived to adulthood.

"Hello, Momma," I replied, and grabbed a box of cheese crackers to put away.

"You bribing them with food. You little shit. They only love you 'cause you feed them that fancy stuff. I can feed my own kids. Don't need you spoilin' 'em," she grumbled as she shuffled her bare feet over to the closest kitchen chair and sat down.

"I'm gonna pay rent before I leave, but I know you have some other bills. Where are they?"

She reached for the pack of cigarettes sitting in the ashtray in the middle of her small brown Formica table. "The bills are on top of the fridge. I hid 'em from Randy. They made him pissy."

Great. The electricity bill and water bill pissed the man off. My mother sure knew how to pick them.

"Oh, Pweston, can I have one of dese now?" Daisy asked, holding up an orange.

"Of course you can. Come here and I'll peel it," I replied, holding out my hand for her to give it to me.

"Stop babying her. You come in here and baby her, then leave, and I'm left to deal with her spoiled ass. She needs to grow up and do shit herself." Momma's bitter words weren't anything new. However, watching Daisy flinch and her eyes fill up with tears I knew she wouldn't shed for fear of getting slapped caused my blood to boil.

I bent down and kissed the top of her head before taking the orange from her and peeling it. Confronting Momma would only make her worse. When I left, it would be up to Jimmy to make sure Daisy was safe. Leaving them here wasn't easy, but I didn't have the kind of money it would take to go to court over it. And the lifestyle I'd chosen in order to make sure they were okay and taken care of wasn't one that the courts would look favorably on. There wasn't a snowball's chance in hell I'd ever get them. The best I could do was come here once a week and feed them and make sure their bills were paid. I couldn't be around Momma more than that.

"When's Daisy's next doctor's appointment?" I asked, wanting to change the subject and find out when I needed to come pick her up and take her.

"I think it's last week. Why don't you call the doc yourself and find out, if you're so damn worried about it. She ain't sick. She's just lazy."

I finished peeling the orange and grabbed a paper towel, then handed it to Daisy.

"Tank you, Pweston."

I knelt down to her level. "You're welcome. Eat that up. It's good for you. I bet Jimmy will go out on the porch with you if you want."

Daisy frowned and leaned forward. "Jimmy won't go outside 'cause Becky Ann lives next doowah. He tinks she's pwetty."

Grinning, I glanced back at Jimmy, whose cheeks were bright red.

"Dammit, Daisy, why you have to go and tell him that?"

"Watch the language with your sister," I warned, and stood up. "Ain't no reason to be embarrassed 'cause you think some girl is good-looking."

"Don't listen to him. He's in a different one's panties ever' night. Just like his daddy was." Momma loved to make me look bad in front of the kids.

Jimmy grinned. "I know. I'm gonna be just like Preston when I grow up."

I slapped him on the back of the head. "Keep it in your pants, boy."

Jimmy laughed and headed for the door. "Come on, Daisy May. I'll go outside with you for a while."

I didn't look back at Momma as I finished putting away the food, then retrieved the bills from the top of the fridge. Brent sat silently on the bar stool, watching me. I would have to spend a little time with him before I left. He was the middle one, the one who didn't push for my attention. I'd sent the other two outside knowing he liked to have me to himself.

"So what's new?" I asked, leaning on the bar across from him.

He smiled and shrugged. "Nothing much. I wanna play football this year, but Momma says it costs too much and I'd be bad at it 'cause I'm scrawny."

God, she was a bitch.

"Is that so? Well, I disagree. I think you'd make an awesome corner or wide receiver. Why don't you get me the info on this and I'll check into it?"

Brent's eyes lit up. "For real? 'Cause Greg and Joe are playing, and they live in the trailers back there." He pointed toward the back of the trailer park. "Their daddy said I could ride with them and stuff. I just needed someone to fill out the paper and pay for it."

"Go on ahead and pay for it. Let him get hurt, and see whose fault it'll be," Momma said through the cigarette hanging out of her mouth.

"I'm sure they have coaches and adults overseeing this so that it is rare someone gets really hurt at this age," I said, shooting a warning glare back at her.

"You're making me raise the sorriest bunch of brats in town.

When they all need bailed outta jail in a few years, that shit is all on you." She stood up and walked back to her room. Once the door slammed behind her, I looked back at Brent.

"Ignore that. You hear me? You're smart, and you're gonna make something of yourself. I believe in you."

Brent nodded. "I know. Thank you for football."

I reached out and patted his head. "You're welcome. Now why don't you come on outside and walk me to my Jeep?"

AMANDA

Marcus, my older brother, was mad at me. He was convinced I was staying home instead of going to Auburn like I'd planned because of Mom. I wasn't. Not really. Well, maybe a little bit. At first it had been for completely selfish reasons. I'd wanted to get Preston Drake to notice me. Well, three months ago I'd gotten my wish for about forty minutes. Since then he hadn't looked my way once. After several pitiful attempts to get his attention, I stopped trying.

Unfortunately, it was a little too late to decide I wanted to go to Auburn instead of the local junior college. I was almost relieved I couldn't go away, though. My mom was dealing with the betrayal and desertion of my dad. He now lived an hour away with his new young girlfriend and their child.

Leaving home meant leaving Mom all alone in this big house. If I hadn't made the decision to stay and try to get Preston's attention, I'd be leaving today for Auburn. Mom would be crying and I would be sick to my stomach with worry. She just wasn't strong enough to be left alone just yet. Maybe next year.

"You can't live here forever, Amanda," Marcus said as he paced in front of me. I had come outside to the pool with the new copy of *People* magazine hoping to get some sun, but Marcus had shown up. "At some point we're going to have to let Mom learn to cope. I know it's hard. Look at me, I'm still stopping by four to five times a week just to make sure she's okay. But I don't want you giving up your dreams because you feel responsible for our mother."

I'd managed to keep my not going away to Auburn a secret from him until today. Normally, he was so wrapped up in his world with his fiancée, Willow, and his online courses to keep up with what I was doing.

"I know this, but maybe I just wasn't ready to leave home. Maybe this is all about me. You ever think of that?"

Marcus frowned and rubbed his chin hard, which meant he was frustrated. "Okay. Fine. Say you don't want to go away just yet. Have you considered maybe going in January? Getting your feet wet with college while at home, then venturing out?"

Sighing, I laid my magazine in my lap. I might as well give up on reading it until he'd gotten this off his chest. "No, I haven't, because that is stupid. I can go an entire year here, then transfer next year. It works for me. I know people here, and I want to be here for the wedding. I want to help Willow plan it. I don't want to be four hours away missing all this."

I'd hit him below the belt. Anything to do with his wedding and he went all soft. Marcus stopped his endless pacing and sat down on the end of the lounge chair beside me. "So this is really about you wanting to stay at home? You're just not ready to leave yet? Because if that is really the case, then I'm good with that. I don't want you going off if you're not ready. Sure as hell don't want you going to Auburn. But if this is what you want—*you* want—then I'm happy. I just don't want what Dad did to take away any more of our lives than it already has."

He was such a good guy. Why couldn't I be infatuated with a good guy like my overprotective, loving brother? There were guys out there like him. I'd met a few. Why did I have to be hung up on a male slut?"

"It *is* all about me. I swear."

Marcus nodded, then slapped my foot before standing back up. "Good. I feel better now. Since you're not moving away today, you're invited to the engagement party the guys are throwing for me and Low."

Guys? "What guys?"

"You know, the guys. Rock, Preston, Dewayne—well, the truth is, mostly Trisha is throwing it and the guys are all planning the alcohol."

"Does she need help?" I asked, thinking how ridiculous it

was that I was asking in hopes that I would be thrown together with Preston in some part of the planning.

"Yeah, I'm sure she does. Why don't you give her a call?"

I would do that. Today. "Okay, cool. When is it?"

"This Friday night."

Want even more Abbi Glines?
Here's a sneak peek at

the vincent brothers

SAWYER

I'd known better than to come here, but I couldn't keep avoiding
the field parties. It was time I started acting as if Beau and Ash
being together didn't bother me.

"Here, man." Ethan shoved a red plastic cup full of beer into
my hand. Frowning, I started to hand it back to him. "Drink it.
You need it. Hell, I need it just watching the three of you."

I was thankful he'd spoken low enough so that no one else
could hear him. I could feel everyone sneaking glances at me.
They were all waiting to see how I would react. It'd been six
months since I'd lost Ash to my brother. It was easier to see
them together now, but normally, I kept my distance. This
was the first time I'd had to witness my horny ass brother kiss
her neck, hand, head, and anything else he could get near his

lips while he carried on a conversation with everyone else and Ashton snuggled up between his legs.

Ethan was right; I needed a drink. Touching the cup to my lips, I tilted my head back and took a very long gulp. Anything to distract me from the make-out session in front of me would be nice.

"I still can't believe you two aren't going to the same college. I always expected y'all to get signed on as a package deal." Toby Horn almost sounded let down that I'd chosen to sign with the University of Florida instead of Alabama, like everyone expected me to. Beau and I had been planning to play for the Crimson Tide since we were five years old. But when Florida had offered me a full ride, I'd taken it. I needed the distance. Ashton was headed to Alabama with Beau, and I just couldn't do it too.

"Florida offered him a sweet deal. Can't blame him for taking it," Beau explained. He got it. He never mentioned it, but he knew why I'd gone with Florida. Beau had been careful for a long time not to shove his relationship with Ashton in my face, but since graduation he'd put that behind him. Every time I saw them lately, she was wrapped up in his arms and he was staring at her with that ridiculous worshipful expression he'd always reserved just for her.

"Alabama can't handle two Vincent boys. I needed to share the love," I replied, focusing my gaze on Toby before taking another swig of my beer.

"It's going to be weird not having you around, though," Ash said. *Damn.* Why'd she have to say anything? Couldn't she sit over there quietly and let Beau paw all over her? Hearing Ashton's voice made it impossible not to lift my eyes to meet her gaze.

The sad tilt of her full lips made that old familiar ache start up in my chest. Only Ashton could get to me this way. "You'll survive. Besides, you two hardly come up for air to notice much of anything else." I'd just sounded like an ass. Ashton's flinch from my snide comment was just another strike against me.

"Careful, Sawyer." The threat in Beau's voice was unmistakable. Silence fell over the group. Everyone's focus was on the two of us. The anger flashing in Beau's glare just pissed me off more. What did he have to be angry about? He had the girl.

"Why don't you calm down? I was responding to her comment. Am I not allowed to speak to her now?"

Beau gripped Ashton's waist and moved her away from him as he stood up. "You got a problem, Sawyer?"

Ashton scrambled to her feet, threw her arms around Beau's neck, and began begging him to ignore me, telling him I didn't mean anything by it, although we both knew I did. Beau's eyes never left mine as he reached behind his neck to unlatch Ashton's hold on him.

As I set my cup down on the bed of my truck, I took a step toward him. This was a fight I needed. Holding my aggression in was so damn hard at times. Ashton, however, wasn't having it. She grabbed Beau's shoulders and jumped up, wrapping her legs firmly around his waist. If seeing her wrapped around him didn't piss me off so bad, I'd laugh at her determination to keep us from fighting. She'd been dealing with us since we were kids, and she knew exactly how to keep us from coming to blows. Throwing herself in the line of fire was the only way.

Amusement lit Beau's eyes as his angry snarl turned into a pleased grin and his eyes shifted from me to Ashton. "What ya doin', baby?" he asked in that slow drawl I hated. He'd been using it on girls since we hit puberty.

"That's the way to distract him, Ash," hooted Kayla Jenkins from Toby's lap.

More catcalls and whistles started. Beau was smiling at her now like she was the most fascinating person in the world. That was it for me. I had to get out of there.

"Let's go get something to eat—I'm starved," Ethan suggested, and Jake North agreed.

"You drive," Ethan called out, and climbed into the passenger seat of my truck. Without looking back at Ash and Beau, I walked around my truck and hopped in. If he hauled her off to his truck, I'd lose it. Leaving was the best idea.

LANA

Jewel flirted outrageously with the bartender. I knew her game and was willing to bet he did too. The brilliant scheme to flash cleavage and bat eyelashes while giggling wasn't the most original idea ever concocted. Why she couldn't just be happy with her soda while we waited for a table was beyond me. The ten-hour road trip I'd been on with her from Alpharetta, Georgia, to southern Alabama fulfilled my quota on quality time spent with my childhood friend and next-door neighbor. Jewel and I had grown up and become two completely different people, but that bond from our childhood had somehow kept us from drifting apart. Still, Jewel could only be endured in small doses.

"Come on, Lana, flash him a view of those fabulous boobs you've finally decided to share with the world," Jewel whispered as her gaze stayed on the young guy fixing drinks for another customer. Shaking my head at her ridiculous request, I picked up my soda and took a sip. I was happy with my soda. If she wanted to make a fool out of herself in hopes of getting a mixed drink, then fine, but I wasn't about to join in. The last thing I needed was to get caught with an alcoholic drink only thirty minutes away from my aunt and uncle's house. My uncle was a Baptist preacher, and if he found out I'd been drinking alcohol, there was no way he'd let me stay with him and his family for the summer.

"You're such a party pooper, Lana," Jewel whined, and glared at my drink like it was offensive.

I didn't really care if she was upset at this point. I just wanted to get some dinner and then get to my aunt and uncle's. The sight of Jewel's taillights driving away was going to be a welcome event.

"I don't get you, Lana. You go and get all gorgeous and finally decide to flaunt what your momma—okay, maybe not your momma because God knows she ain't real attractive; how about flaunt what luck must have given you?—and for what? Nothing! That's what! You buy yourself a new, sexy, cute wardrobe and get a hairstyle to show off that head of hair of yours, but you *never* flirt. It's as if you did this for yourself, and that's just dumb. Guys notice you now, Lana. They turn their heads, but you just ignore them."

This was a familiar tirade of hers. It drove her nuts that I didn't throw myself at any boy who looked my way. I wasn't about to tell her the reason why. That kind of information would make Jewel dangerous. She'd find a way to ruin everything. She wouldn't mean to, of course, but she would. Her loud mouth always seemed to bring a world of trouble with it.

"I've told you that I'm just not interested in dating right now. We just graduated. I want a summer to prepare for college in the fall, enjoy being away from my insane mother, and just—relax."

Jewel sighed and bent her head down to nibble on her straw while her eyes zeroed in on the poor bartender who must have been about ready for us to be seated at a table.

"You can still come with me, you know. Skip this living-with-the-preacher stuff and come party all summer at the beach. Corey would love you to join us. Her stepfather's condo has three bedrooms and a killer view of the ocean."

A summer hanging out with a drunken Jewel and friends was not appealing at all. I had my plans, and so far everything I'd put into motion was running smoothly. But I couldn't help but be nervous about the next step. It was the most crucial.

Having my naturally red hair darkened to a deep copper and styled attractively instead of pulled back in a braid or ponytail had been step one. The darker red color had made my pale skin seem almost delicate. Then the cleaning out of my closet had been the next move. I'd bagged up every single piece of clothing I owned and dropped it off at the local Goodwill. My mother had been horrified, but after she'd seen the clothing style I intended to replace it with, she'd been very supportive. Unlike most mothers, my mother wanted to see me in shorts that showed off almost all my legs and tight tops that emphasized my c-cup boobs.

Jewel had wanted to teach me how to apply makeup, but I'd kindly refused and went to the Clinique counter at Macy's and had them teach me. Then I'd bought everything they'd used. Although I'd never been one for makeup, I had to agree that it did startling things to my eyes. I'd closed my bedroom door and stared at myself in fascination for hours after they'd put makeup on me.

Convincing my mother to let me stay the summer with my aunt and uncle had been a little more difficult. My cousin Ashton had helped tremendously with this part. She'd talked to her mother who in return talked to mine. Our mothers are sisters, and once my aunt convinced my mother that Ashton truly wanted me to come spend our last summer before college together, I'd been so excited I'd momentarily forgotten about the last step in the plan, the reason why I'd made myself moderately attractive and begged to come stay the summer with my cousin. The goal sounded so simple, but when I allowed myself to dwell on it then, it became so incredibly complicated. Getting a boy to fall head-over-heels in love with you wasn't easy—especially when he'd been in love with your cousin for as long as you could remember.

ABBI GLINES is the author of *The Vincent Boys* and *The Vincent Brothers* in addition to several other YA novels. A devoted book lover, Abbi lives with her family in Alabama. She maintains a Twitter addiction at @abbiglines and can also be found at AbbiGlines.com.